THE ONTARIO TRILLIUM FOUNDATION **LA FONDATION TRILLIUM DE L'ONTARIO**

The Ontario Trillium Foundation, an agency of the Ministry of
Culture, receives annually $100 million of government funding
generated through Ontario's charity casino initiative.

'Isla.'

When she didn't answer, Salvador moved into the en suite bathroom and she lay there, staring at his reflection in the dressing room table mirror, watching as he quietly undressed and then leant over the sink to brush his teeth. The vivid raised scar on his back, so red and angry, was easy to make out even from this distance.

How she longed to touch it, longed to run gentle fingers over it, to ask him how much it hurt, wincing as she imagined the gnarled metal from the car wreckage stabbing into his beautiful back and then the torturous operation to remove it.

But their wounds didn't only lie skin-deep. Now they had to fight for the survival of their marriage!

A&E DRAMA

Blood pressure is high and pulses are racing
in these fast-paced dramatic stories
from Mills & Boon® Medical Romance™.
They'll move a mountain
to save a life in an emergency, be they
the crash team, emergency doctors, or
paramedics. There are lots of critical
engagements amongst the high tensions
and emotional passions in these exciting stories
of lives and loves at risk!

*Carol Marinelli now also writes
for Modern Romance™!*

Don't miss her latest exciting story
HIS PREGNANT MISTRESS

On sale next month!

Recent titles by the same author:

Medical Romance™

THE DOCTOR'S OUTBACK BABY
(*Tennengarrah Clinic*)
THE BUSH DOCTOR'S CHALLENGE
(*Tennengarrah Clinic*)
THE BABY EMERGENCY
(*Tennengarrah Clinic*)

Modern Romance™

THE ITALIAN'S MARRIAGE BARGAIN
THE BILLIONAIRE'S CONTRACT BRIDE

EMERGENCY:
A MARRIAGE
WORTH KEEPING

BY
CAROL MARINELLI

MILLS & BOON and
MILLS & BOON with the Rose Device
are registered trademarks of the publisher.

First published in Great Britain 2005
Large Print edition 2005
Harlequin Mills & Boon Limited,
Eton House, 18-24 Paradise Road,
Richmond, Surrey TW9 1SR

© The SAL Marinelli Family Trust 2005

ISBN 0 263 18476 5

Set in Times Roman 17 on 19½ pt.
17-0905-45619

Printed and bound in Great Britain
by Antony Rowe Ltd, Chippenham, Wiltshire

PROLOGUE

'Does your husband have a temper?'

'He's Spanish,' Isla answered, thinking of that gorgeous, volatile Latin temperament, of Sav's arms waving in exasperation as he tried to ram home a point, tripping over the words as his mother tongue took over. 'So of course he's got a temper.' Isla gave a nervous smile but it faded as she saw the solicitor's eyebrow lift a good inch. 'But he's never hit me,' she broke in immediately, annoyed at the connotation. 'Sav would never hit me—never,' she said again for effect, but the solicitor remained unmoved.

'He doesn't have to hit you,' Karin said knowingly. 'Abuse isn't always physical.'

'I'm not abused,' Isla said firmly.

'But your husband *does* have a temper?'

'Actually, having said that, he doesn't have a temper any more.' Isla let out a low, mirthless laugh. 'We've moved well past the stand-up row stage.'

'And where are you now, Isla?' Karin asked, waiting patiently as Isla took her time to respond, wondering how she could sum up in a short sentence the abyss their marriage had fallen into, the long lonely days rattling around a house that was too big, too quiet, followed by even longer, lonely nights as they lay in bed, firmly entrenched on their own sides and pretending to be asleep.

'Where are you now, Isla?' Karin asked again, only more gently this time, watching as her client's tired, reddened eyes slowly lifted.

'Sitting in a solicitor's office, working out my options.'

The silence dragged on, Isla immersed in her own thoughts and Karin waiting for her client to elaborate further. Usually an expert at summing up people, to Karin there was something about Isla Ramirez that didn't add up. When she'd walked nervously into her office two weeks ago Karin had been positive that after the initial brief consultation she'd never see her again. Sure almost that the rather fragile-looking blonde with the perfectly manicured nails and Pilate-toned thighs had arrived at the solicitor's office on the back of a marital row. The affection in her voice when she'd spoken about her husband hadn't fitted the usual mould of a woman about to leave her husband, and when Karin had actually gone through the procedures for a divorce, she had been sure that Isla Ramirez would be out of her office never to be seen again, yet here she was two weeks later, a touch thinner, a touch more exhausted perhaps, but with a steely determination Karin had missed at their last meeting.

It was Karin who eventually broke the silence, picking up her pen and shuffling the pile of notices in front of her. 'OK, so we'll lodge your application citing irretrievable breakdown?'

The solicitor's pen was poised over her notes

and Isla knew she was waiting for her to respond. Clearing her throat, Isla attempted to say yes but had to settle instead for a hesitant nod, which Karin Jensen failed to notice.

'That is what we agreed on?' Karin checked, looking up when Isla still failed to answer.

She hadn't exactly agreed on anything, Isla wanted to point out. She'd merely come in to discuss her options.

Again.

Admittedly, the first visit had been a rather pale affair, with herself mumbling questions, feeling as guilty as hell for even being there, and the solicitor determinedly not giving too much away during the utterly no-obligation, free consultation.

Karin had been much more animated on this visit. Now there was actually money on the table, now she'd seemingly passed from curious to determined, Karin was only too happy to discuss Isla's options.

Only too happy to sum up nine years of marriage in two little words.

Two very apt little words, Isla reluctantly admitted, fiddling with her handbag and hoping Karin would offer her another glass of water.

Her marriage had definitely broken down.

And if Sav even had a hint she'd visited a solicitor, irretrievable was certainly a word that sprang to mind.

'I don't want to do anything just yet.' Her voice was back and Isla deliberately ignored the frown flickering across the young woman's face. 'I'm going back to work tomorrow and once I've got a wage coming in and have found somewhere for the children and me to live—'

'Hold it right there.' Karin put up a very steady hand, a sharp contrast to Isla's trembling ones fiddling nervously in her lap. 'The last thing you do is go back to work. Salvador, I mean Sav, has an obligation to you and the children to keep you in the style to which you're accustomed, and as for moving out…' She shook her head very slowly, very deliberately and fixed her client with a steely glare.

'It's your husband that will be moving out of the family home.'

'I don't want it to be like that,' Isla insisted. 'I have no intention of kicking him out of his home. Sav has enough on his plate already, without looking for somewhere else to live. He's an emergency consultant. He hasn't got time to be—'

'And you're a mother to his twin sons,' Karin broke in. 'It makes more sense for Salv—Sav to move out than to traumatize the boys with a house move as well as a divorce.'

'Perhaps,' Isla sighed.

'And the very last thing you should even be thinking about is returning to work. It's up to Sav to support you, to keep you in a manner—'

'And he will,' Isla broke in. 'I don't doubt that for a moment. But I'm more than capable of working, I certainly don't need to bleed him dry. I know that when he calms down he'll do the right thing and provide for me and the children.'

'Maybe he will.' Karin shrugged but her voice hardened. 'For a while perhaps, at least until the next Mrs Ramirez comes along.'

'Sav's not like that,' Isla said—immediately and with conviction. 'There's no one else involved in this, and I really can't see anyone else "coming along"—for either of us,' she added, but even though Karin never turned as much as a hair, never said a single word, Isla could almost hear the *Just you wait* that hung in the air, and it infuriated her.

What would Karin Jensen know about them?

What would Karin Jensen know about the love that had been between them, the sheer magic they had shared, and if, even with all that love, this marriage couldn't work, then there was no way on this earth she'd do it again and she knew, just knew, that Sav would feel the same.

'I want this divorce to be as amicable as possible…'

'There's no such thing.' Karin shook her head. 'Not when there are children involved.

How do you know that Sav isn't going to apply for custody of the boys? How do you know that Sav isn't going to want to be the primary carer?'

Isla felt the colour drain out of her cheeks.

'As soon as these papers are served the first thing Sav's going to do is get himself a solicitor and, believe me, Isla, once that happens you can leave the word amicable out of your vocabulary for a while. You need to come out of your corner fighting.'

'But Sav hasn't done anything wrong,' Isla protested.

'Then why are you here?'

She had a point, Isla reluctantly acknowledged. At every turn she'd defended Sav, at every opportunity she'd insisted how nice he was, what a wonderful father he was, what a great provider he'd been. But as much as it galled her to admit it, Karin had a point: if her marriage was so wonderful, why at two o'clock on a Wednesday afternoon was she sitting in a solicitor's office in the city, trying to find out how a seemingly happily married woman went about getting a divorce?

'Because I can't live with him any more.' Tears she'd been determined not to shed in this meeting were threatening now, and Isla blinked them back, expecting an irritated sigh from the well-groomed businesswoman that sat on the other side of the table. But instead Karin pushed over a box of tissues and poured another cup of water from the cooler as Isla did her best to regain her composure. 'Because nothing I do or say seems to make a difference. We just don't talk…'

'Since Casey died?'

This time Isla didn't even try to blink back her tears, they were coming thick and fast just at the mention of her son's name—a name she ached to hear, a name that was curiously absent in her household, a name that brought a warning look from Sav every time she ventured it.

'I know he misses him. I know that he's devastated at what happened, but he won't talk to me about it. He won't talk to me about anything any more. It's like living with a stranger.'

'Look, I'm not one to knock back business.' Karin gave a dry smile but her eyes were kind. 'But it sounds to me as if there's still a lot of love there. Have you thought about counselling?' She watched Isla screw up her nose.

'Sav doesn't believe in it.'

'But he's a doctor,' Karin responded. 'Surely—'

'It's a case of do as I say, not as I do with Sav. Sure, he recommends it for his patients, and no doubt he believes in its merits, but he's too damn proud and stubborn to even contemplate that counselling might help him.'

'Have you been to see anyone?'

Isla nodded. 'I don't think I'd be here otherwise,' she said with simple honesty. 'It definitely helped at first.'

'But not now?'

Isla shook her head as Karin let out a tiny sigh. 'I've gone as far as I can on my own with this. Things really have to change at home.

Have to change,' she reiterated. 'And I just can't see any other way.'

'Talk to him again, Isla. Tell him how close he is to losing—'

'I've been trying to for over a year now,' Isla gulped, 'and I get nowhere. If it was just about me, then perhaps I could take it. But it's affecting the twins, I know it is. As much as we try to act normal in front of them, they can feel the tension between us. They've been through so much already.'

'A divorce isn't an easy option,' Karin pointed out. 'No matter how gently you tread, this will affect them.'

'I know.' Isla nodded, closing her eyes in dread, appalled that it had come to this, appalled at what she was instigating. 'But I've given it a lot of thought.' She gave a painful laugh, utterly void of humour. 'In fact, it's all I've thought about. I honestly believe that in the long term this will be for the best. A new start, a clean break for all of us. Not the torture of the boys watching their parents' marriage slowly fall apart, the unspoken rule that they can never say their brother's name in front of their father. They miss him as much as we do, and Sav's silence on the subject isn't helping. It's making it worse, so much worse than it has to be. It's like a cancer invading every cell of our lives.' She blew her nose loudly into the tissues, her head spinning as she tried to process all Karin had said about the mechanics of a divorce. Trying and failing to contemplate a future, however bleak the present might be, without Sav.

'Have you given any thought to a trial separation?' Karin suggested. 'Say, three months apart…'

'Sav wouldn't hear of it.' Instantly Isla shook her head. 'If he even knew that I was here, it would be all over bar the shouting. It's all or nothing with Sav, and frankly I don't think it would be fair on the children, leaving them in limbo for three months. If I go ahead with this, it has to be a clean break.'

'OK,' Karin said slowly. 'Then why don't we

schedule another appointment?' The solicitor's voice was calm and even, such a contrast to the swirling, confusing mass of emotions Isla seemed to be constantly engulfed in these days. 'Say, for a month's time?'

'Why?' Isla blinked back at the other woman. 'What's that going to solve? I didn't come here on a whim, Karin.'

'I'm sure you didn't,' Karin said sympathetically. 'But we have gone over a lot of ground today, there's a lot of information there for you to process. Think about it,' she said firmly. 'Think long and hard about it, and while you're at it try talking to Sav again, tell him how close he is to the marriage ending.'

'I thought you were a divorce lawyer…' Isla managed a wobbly smile '…not a marriage counsellor.'

'I'm a *great* divorce lawyer,' Karin fixed her with a steely glare. 'I fight for my clients to the last breath, but at the end of the day, I need them on my side.' She gave a small shrug. 'I'm just not quite sure that you're there yet.'

'I'm not,' Isla admitted, raking a hand through her newly cut blonde hair and feeling foolish all of a sudden. 'I've wasted your time—' Isla started, but Karin waved her apology away.

'Not at all, Isla. You're the one paying for my advice, so take it. Go home, think about what I've said and try again to talk to Sav. If you still want to go ahead with a divorce, I'll be here for you and more than ready to roll.'

'Thank you.'

Karin stood up and shook her client's hand. 'But you will listen to what I've said and not go and do anything stupid, though?'

'Like what?' Isla frowned.

'Like moving out and starting a job.' She gave a low laugh. 'Hair and nails and a figure like that don't come cheap, Isla.'

Isla shook her head. 'I do my own nails, Karin, and as for the figure, you're right—it didn't come cheap.' She watched as the solicitor frowned. 'Losing a child is the highest price anyone can pay.' Opening the door to the office, she paused a moment. 'This is my divorce, Karin. I'll do it my way.'

Her bravado evaporated as soon as Isla stepped into the waiting room. Waiting in line at Reception behind an irate fair-headed gentleman who was insisting that he be seen next, furiously demanding an explanation for a summons he had received that morning, Isla felt as if she were drowning in her own misery, being pulled ever deeper into a circle of hate where she and Sav surely didn't belong.

One month.

Amazingly it calmed her.

One month to get her life in order, one month to give her marriage yet another shot, one month to come to her decision.

CHAPTER ONE

'WHAT did you do today?'

Cheeks flaming, Isla took another slug of water, every drop sticking in her throat as she attempted to eat the dinner she had hastily prepared for Sav and herself. Late picking the boys up from school, the whole evening had been a downward spiral of chaos, but thankfully Sav had been caught up at work, finally coming home late to a reasonable tidy house and a seemingly normal wife. The twins, delighted after their rare treat of take-away burgers and chips, were supposed to be in bed, but she could hear them bumping around upstairs and for once was grateful for it, grateful that Sav left the table to sort them out and didn't seem to notice her discomfort.

'I said they could read for ten more minutes.' He didn't come back to the table. Instead, he headed for the fridge and pulled out a bottle of wine, pouring her a glass before sitting down.

'Have one,' she suggested, but Sav shook his head.

'The hospital might call.'

'You're not on call tonight Sav,' Isla pointed out, 'and even if they do, surely you can have one glass with dinner.'

'So, what did you do today?' Sav asked again, ignoring what she had just said, and getting back to a subject she'd rather ignore.

'Not much.' Isla gave a vague shrug. 'I had my hair done this morning.'

'It looks nice,' Sav responded, barely even looking up, and Isla managed a wry smile at the solicitor's comments—this morning had been her first trip to the hairdresser's in over a year, her long dark blonde hair finally meeting scissors for the first time since Casey's death. The trim she'd intended before she started back to work had inadvertently turned into her own extreme make-over—her hair now hung in a sleek shoulder-length curtain and she'd taken the hair-dresser's advice and had a few foils put in. The hairdresser had raved at the result, and even the mums at the school had jumped up and down as Isla had stood blushing at the scrutiny but quietly pleased. But the one opinion that mattered, the one person she'd been hoping to impress, had scarcely even noticed.

'What else?'

'Not much.' Isla blushed. A useless liar at the best of times, she wondered how some people managed to have affairs, managed to spend an afternoon making steamy, breathless love and somehow managing to arrive at the dinner table apparently normal. Her two trips to see Karin Jensen had been fraught with guilt—paying in cash, ringing them up to ensure they'd understood that no correspondence should be sent to the house. Even her parking ticket for the Art Centre in Melbourne had been carefully shredded.

Oh, God!

Another lurch of panic as she remembered her E-Tag, the tiny white box that Melburnians displayed on the dashboards of their cars, the tiny white box that bleeped as you went through the road tolls on the way to the city. If Sav looked at the bill he'd know she'd been there, would…

Taking another slug of wine, she ignored Sav's slightly questioning glance as he topped up her glass, knowing he was undoubtedly confused. It normally took her the best part of an evening to work her way down a single glass, but here she was two minutes in and practically on her second!

He wouldn't even look at the E-Tag account when it arrived, Isla consoled herself, and even if he did, as if he'd remember what had happened the previous month, as if he'd demand to know what the hell she'd been doing in the city that day. Sav wasn't like that.

They trusted each other.

Tears pierced her eyes as she realized the incongruity of her thoughts.

Never in a million years would it enter his

head that she'd been to see a solicitor today. That their marriage was nearly at the end of the line.

'It suits you.'

'Sorry?' Blinking back at him, she tried to drag her mind back to the conversation but lost her way.

'Your hair.' He gave her a rare smile. 'You're upset that I didn't notice you'd had it cut.'

'I'm not!'

'But I did notice,' he carried on, ignoring her denial. 'As soon as I came in I thought how nice it looked. I just forgot to say it.'

Which just about summed them up really, Isla thought sadly. 'I picked up my uniforms from the hospital as well. I called in to see you but you were tied up with a patient. I told them not to disturb you.'

'It's been like that all day—all week, actually.' Looking up, Isla could see the lines of tension grooved around his dark eyes as he spoke. His black hair, which to most people probably looked immaculate, by Sav's high standards was probably overdue for a trim, and she realized how tired he looked—not the usual, it's-been-a-long-day tired, but totally, completely exhausted. 'I'd better get used to it, I guess. I've got Heath questioning my every move, taking great pains to point out every T I don't cross or I that I don't dot in an attempt to show how much better he'd have been for the consultant's role, and with Martin not due back for another three weeks it's going to be hell.'

The problems with Heath had been an ongoing saga since Sav had been made consultant. Sav and Heath had both applied for the consultant's position eighteen months ago, and both of them had agreed at the time, 'May the best man win.' But when the position had gone to Sav, mainly due to the unspoken fact that Heath had been going through a messy divorce and custody issues, Heath had taken it in bad part, taking an almost morbid delight in pointing out how much better a choice he'd have been for the job when Sav had taken a month off after Casey's death.

'Hell!' Sav added just for effect, and Isla knew that little tag had been aimed at her. It wasn't just Heath that was getting to Sav. Isla had lived with him long enough to read between the lines. Taking a breath, she decided to voice what was clearly on his mind.

'And me going back to work isn't exactly going to help matters.'

'I didn't say that,' Sav snapped.

'No, but you thought it,' Isla retorted, taking an angry sip of her wine. 'You don't start till nine, Sav. The boys' uniforms will be out, I'll give them their breakfast before I go. All you have to do is drop them off at school—it's hardly a big deal.'

'It is a big deal if you're having a heart attack,' Sav retorted, his Spanish accent deepening the angrier he got. 'It's one hell of a big deal if you're lying there bleeding to death in Resuscitation and the only consultant covering the department is at home, babysitting his children.'

'If that happens,' Isla responded, trying desperately to keep her voice even, 'then you'll ring Louise. She's only around the corner, she's said that she'll come straightaway. We've already worked this out!'

'No, you worked it out, Isla. You're the one who worked this whole harebrained scheme out, you're the one who decided to make your grand return to nursing the one month in the year when you know Martin Elmes is on holiday.'

'There was never going to be a good time for you, Sav,' Isla retorted. 'The simple fact of the matter is that you don't want me to go back to work, least of all as a nurse in *your* department. You have this archaic belief that any wife of yours should be firmly entrenched at home.'

'That's not true.' Sav shook his head, pushed away his half-eaten dinner then shook his head again. 'The plan was that you were going to go back to work next year—'

'No,' Isla broke in, 'the plan was, once the children were at school I'd start back at work.' It was Isla pushing her plate away now, Isla who couldn't face another morsel, Isla trying to raise another subject that was out of bounds. 'And the children *are* at school now. It would have been next year if…'

He was standing up now, ready to stalk off to the study or the living room, to pick up the phone and ring the hospital and hopefully find out that he had to go in. And on any other night, Isla would have followed him in, finished what she was saying, tried to force the conversation, but tonight she let him go, tonight she just let him walk off, because quite simply she didn't have the energy to scrape at the stony walls of silence he so forcibly erected.

Just couldn't do this any more.

'I'm going for a run after I've tidied the kitchen,' she was shouting into the hallway as he stalked off, and Isla saw his shoulders stiffen, an almost questioning look on that inscrutable face as he turned around, her lack of response clearly not what he'd expected. 'I'll take my mobile. You can call me if the hospital rings and I'll come straight back.'

Sav didn't call. In fact, he didn't even come out of the study when she arrived home a good hour later, and barely looked up when, drooping with exhaustion, she popped her head around the study door and said goodnight.

She should have fallen asleep. Only half an hour ago she'd barely been able to keep her eyes open, but the shower had woken her, her mind spinning with guilt as she lay in bed, scarcely able to fathom where she had been today, reeling in horror as she pictured Sav's face if he ever found out, tears slipping into her hair as she imagined the devastation on Luke's and Harry's faces if they ever had to break it to them that Mummy and Daddy wouldn't be living together any more.

'Isla?' Sav whispered it gently as he tiptoed into the bedroom and Isla recognized the low throaty, unvoiced question.

At first, when Casey had died, their love life had been put on hold. They had clung to each other through the long dark nights more out of fear than intimacy, guilt impinging on guilt whenever passion had taken over, as if somehow it had been wrong to feel pleasure, to indulge each other. But as their marriage had dissolved around them as the communication gates had slammed firmly closed, still, surprisingly perhaps, the passion had remained, the huge sexual attraction that had sparked on contact all those years ago still burning brightly, the one shining light in their marriage apart from the twins. It was the only time Sav let his guard down, the sweet, sweet release of their lovemaking almost addictive in its nature, everything else temporarily cast aside as passion took over.

But not tonight.

Yes, she was going to give her marriage all she had, but the physical side of it wasn't the issue. The physical side of it was the only bit that didn't need rescuing.

'Isla.' He said it again, and when she didn't answer, Sav moved into the *en suite* and she lay there staring at his reflection in the dressing-table mirror, watching as Sav quietly undressed then leant over the sink to brush his teeth, the vivid raised scar on his back so red and angry it was easy to make out even from this distance.

How she longed to touch it, longed to run gentle fingers over it, to ask him how much it hurt, wincing as she imagined the gnarled metal from the car wreckage stabbing into his beautiful back, the intricate operation to remove it.

Closing her eyes as the light flicked off, she concentrated on keeping her breathing even, willed her hammering heart to slow down as he came across the room and pulled the sheet back, felt the indentation of the mattress as he climbed in. She waited for him to roll over, to turn his back to her, only he didn't. This time a strong arm reached out in the darkness, his body spooning in beside her, his face burying itself in her hair and inhaling the unfamiliar citrus scent of the hairdresser's shampoo. She could feel his arousal nudging into the backs of her thighs, his hand dusting over the curve of her bottom. She could feel the stirring of her own arousal somewhere deep inside, her body responding just as it always did, her nipples jutting to attention at the mere suggestion of his touch. And it hurt, physically hurt, not to respond, to lie there feigning sleep when every nerve, every pore screamed for his touch, when her mind begged for the balmy oblivion only Sav could bring. But she couldn't do it, couldn't make love to him given where she'd been today.

Couldn't pretend any more, even for a little while, that everything was OK.

CHAPTER TWO

'YOU look nice, Mum!' Luke, as blond and as sunny-natured as his mother had once been, smiled up from the table as Isla poured milk over his cereal, lisping the words through the huge gap where his four front teeth used to be.

'It's my new uniform,' Isla answered, glancing down at the navy trousers and pale pink polo top, a far cry from the starched white dress that had been the order of the day seven years ago, the same white dress she'd worn on her occasional casual shift to keep her nursing registration up to date. And even though Luke was completely and utterly biased and thought that his mother, no matter how she looked, was absolutely gorgeous, this morning Isla half agreed with him.

She felt nice.

OK, the blonde silk curtain hadn't survived her evening run and two showers, but she'd piled it high in a ponytail on her head, added a dash of rouge to her pale cheeks and, given it was her first day, had gone the whole hog and put on mascara and a slick of pale lipstick. The image that had greeted her when she'd stared in the mirror had for once been pleasing.

She looked thirty.

OK, most thirty-year-olds didn't want to look thirty, but for Isla it was as if she'd knocked off a decade in one hit. The agony of the past months had left their mark. Her natural good looks seemed to have faded into the shadowy greys of grief—not that it had even entered her head as appearances were way down on her list of priorities when it was an effort just to breathe, a physical effort to prepare the twins' lunches, to paint on a smile when she got up in the morning, the endless hours between four and seven when her grief was put on hold to give the twins the mother they needed. But finally, after all this time, despite the agony of her personal life the proverbial silver lining was if not shining through then glowing on the edges occasionally. The odd spontaneous laugh at something on television, even managing to listen without drifting off when her friend Louise banged on about the war against cellulite. Tiny milestones perhaps, but to Isla they were monumental—and now she was wearing make-up.

'What do you think, Harry?'

Harry didn't answer, his dark hair sticking up at all angles. He merely scowled into his cereal and carried on eating, a mini-version of his father in both looks and personality, though fortunately at this young age he was a lot easier to read than the larger version.

'I'm only going to be working three days a week, Harry,' Isla said, picking up her coffee cup and taking five minutes she really didn't have this morning to sit down at the breakfast table. 'Mondays, Thursdays and Fridays—and even on those days I'll be finished in plenty of time to pick you up from school.'

'But you're not going to *take* us to school,' Harry pointed out, managing somehow to load a simple statement with a hefty dose of guilt. Another wave of panic seemed to rush in. If even this small change to his routine was causing his little world to rock, what would it be like if—?

Not now!

Forcibly Isla pushed that thought out of her mind. There was enough to be dealt with this morning, without dwelling on the bigger picture.

'But Daddy will take you!' Isla responded in a falsely cheerful voice. 'Won't that be fun?'

'Not if he has to go to work as well,' Harry said accusingly. 'Then we'll have to go to Louise's.'

'You like going to Louise's,' Isla said, feeling as if her face might crack, and realizing suddenly that the words *Daddy* and *Mummy* were no longer in the twins' vocabulary, another sign if she'd needed one that they were growing up fast.

'I like going to Louise's *after* school,' Harry said with such a dry edge to his voice that Isla half expected Sav to look up from the cereal bowl. 'I want you to take me.'

'Harry, I can't,' Isla said firmly. 'Because I have to work.'

'Why?'

A perfect mum would have answered the eternal question, Isla thought, closing her eyes in exasperation. A perfect mum would have taken yet another five minutes out of an already rushed morning and come up with some impromptu speech about the merits of a work ethic, that even though they didn't need the money, sick people still needed nurses and that even though Mummy loved him very much, Mummy had a brain that wasn't quite stretched enough practising her serve at the local tennis club.

Only this perfect mum seemed to have hung up her apron strings, Isla thought darkly. How could she begin to explain to Harry the real truth? Not just about his parents' marriage, but the long, lonely days rattling around a house that was too big, too empty without a little boy that should be getting ready to go to kinder now? Who could she tell, who would begin to understand the loneliness, the panic, the agony that gripped her when everyone had left? How she lay for hours on Casey's bed, staring at the ceiling, trying to inhale his sweet pudgy scent, imagining those reddish curls on the pillow beside her, whispering stories into the air and praying he could hear…

'Why?' Harry asked again, and Isla took a deep breath, swallowed the tears that were always close and stood up. 'Why do you have to go to work?'

'Because I do, Harry.'

Not the best answer, but the best she could do today.

'Will it be fun?' Luke poured himself a glass of orange juice, and managed to get more on the table than in his glass. 'Working with Dad?'

'I guess, though I'm sure we'll both be so busy that we'll hardly see each other.'

Who was she kidding?

Loading up the dishwasher, not for the first time Isla questioned the wisdom of going to work alongside Sav, especially given the fact that in a few short weeks their marriage might be over, but it had been the only way to get back into nursing. There may well be an impossible shortage of nurses, but nothing had been done to make the shifts more parent-friendly. OK, there was a cre`che at the hospital, but because Luke and Harry were way past that now, it didn't help matters for Isla. Late shifts were out of the question— she could hardly land Louise with two boisterous twins for three evenings a week, and as for night shifts, with the amount of times Sav was called to the hospital in the small hours, it quite simply didn't even merit a mention.

The emergency room had been the only department willing to offer her three early shifts, and, no doubt, the fact her husband was the consultant there had been an influencing factor. Still, Isla had consoled herself when she had accepted the job, there was a new hospital opening up nearby in a few weeks. Every time they drove past the once massive empty field, another wing seemed to have been put on. They were up to concreting the ambulance bay and according to the local paper they would be recruiting staff within a month. Once her foot was back in the door, once she was earning a wage and had her confidence back, she could put in an application there.

'OK, I'm off.' Kissing the boys, Isla forced another bright smile. 'Dad's just gone to get dressed and then he'll be down.'

'Mum?' Harry's single word stopped her in her tracks. She could almost hear the fear behind it, see the confusion in his guarded eyes as Isla threw her mental clock in the bin and walked back over to him. 'Will it be fun? For Dad, I mean. Do you think you going to work with him will make him happier?'

Oh, God. If Sav heard this it would kill him,

Isla thought with a stab of pain that was physical. He tried so hard to hide it, tried so hard to paint on a smile when the kids were around, but seeing the torture, the utter angst in Harry's eyes only confirmed to Isla that change, however hard it might be at the time, was definitely needed.

This was affecting them all.

'*You* make Daddy happy,' Isla said softly. 'You *and* Luke.'

'And you!' Luke chimed in, but there was a tiny wobble in his voice that didn't bear thinking about.

'Come on.' Isla smiled. 'Finish up your breakfast and then you can brush your teeth.'

Darting up the stairs and into the bedroom, she hovered by the bathroom door, watching as Sav ran the electric razor over his morning shadow, a dark towel hung low around his hips, the *en suite* still steamed up from his prolonged shower earlier. That delicious male scent hung in the air. It still turned her to jelly, and for an indulgent moment she watched the impossibly wide shoulders tapering into lean hips, the dark olive skin, swarthy yet soft, scarcely able to fathom that even after nine years of marriage, even after all they had been through, were still going through, just a glimpse of him in an unguarded moment could have this sort of impact on her.

'Are you going now?'

Blushing, realizing she'd been caught staring, Isla nodded.

'The boys are just finishing their breakfast, their clothes and schoolbags are—'

'We'll manage fine.'

'I know.' She gave a tiny shrug. 'Luke seems fine, Harry's a bit—'

'He'll be OK,' Sav broke in again. 'Don't worry.'

'I am worried, though, Sav. Harry's upset, not just about me working—'

'Harry's got too much Mediterranean blood in his veins for his own good.' Again Sav halted her. 'He wants his mother home in the kitchen, worrying about him all day long.'

She knew he'd meant it as a joke. Sav was fiercely proud of his heritage, adored Spain, missed it more than he ever let on, knowing Isla felt guilty for all he had given up to marry her. But even if it had been a joke, there was a semblance of truth behind it, and Isla chose to pursue it.

'What about you, Sav?'

She watched his shoulders stiffen slightly, waited as he splashed some aftershave into his hands and slapped it on before slowly turning around to face her.

'I'd rather you were at home, too.' He stared directly at her, dark eyes boring into her, honesty behind every word. 'But not because I'm a chauvinist, Isla.'

'Then why?'

'You're going to be late.'

'Sav, please, tell me—'

'Isla, it's your first day. If you're really serious about going back to work then now isn't the time for an in-depth discussion.' He was right, and if he'd left it there it would have been OK. But Sav had to get the last word in, had to spoil yet another morning with his own immovable view on things. 'Anyway…' He stalked out of the *en suite*, ripped off his towel and somehow managed to pull on his boxers and still look haughty at the same time. 'What I think doesn't really come into it. You've made that perfectly clear. You've made your choice: you're doing whatever it is you need to do, Isla. The rest of us will just have to work around it.'

'You're impossible, Sav. You make it sound as if I'm off to a nightclub, or abandoning you all for a week in Bali to have massages and facials and lie on a beach, while I leave you all to fend for yourselves. I'm going to work, for heaven's sake.'

'Then go.'

Without another word she turned around, marched down the stairs, absolutely refusing to look back, determined not to make this wretched morning any worse.

'Isla.' Sav was at the top of the stairs, and slowly she turned to face him. 'Good luck.'

Damn!

Why did he have to go and do that? Isla thought. Why did he have to go and do the right thing, say something so nice, when they both knew he didn't want her to go back?

'Thanks.'

They met halfway down the stairs. 'You'll be fine.'

'I hope so.' Isla sniffed.

'I know so.' He picked up the name tag that hung around her neck, staring at the security photo for a moment, and Isla felt her breath catch in her throat as his fingers dusted over her chest, the sudden intimacy unfamiliar and un-expected. 'You were Isla Howard last time we worked together. Isla Howard, a grad nurse with an attitude.'

'And you were the visiting overseas registrar that the whole department promptly fell in love with.'

'Good times,' Sav said softly, and she nodded, dragging her eyes up to meet his.

'Very.' Isla gulped, terrified of saying the wrong thing, pushing too hard, not wanting this fragile moment to end, relishing this tiny, unexpected tender moment. But just as the past caught up, just as she glimpsed again the man she had once known, the shutters snapped closed, just the briefest of kisses brushing her cheek as he took a step back up the stairs. 'You'd better go.'

'Bye,' Isla said quickly, darting out of the door, trying for both their sakes to escape the horrible gap in their conversation, the parting ritual that had fallen by the wayside fourteen months ago.

Drive safely.

They'd always said it, always hugged each other at the door as one of them had been leaving, whispered the words to whoever had been driving. But like so much else it was another thing out of bounds.

Sav, no doubt, felt he'd lost the right to say

it, Isla thought as she climbed into her car and started the engine, and in turn how could she say it to him? Sav would take it as a warning, an accusation even.

It hadn't been his fault.

None of this was anyone's fault, Isla knew that, knew that, knew that!

She had told herself over and over and had begged, *begged* Sav to accept that fact.

'The wrong place at the wrong time' had been the coroner's exact words.

No one could have foreseen, least of all Sav, that the car heading towards them had been a time bomb about to explode. Even the poor driver couldn't have known that as he'd headed along the dual carriageway, the heart attack he'd been dreading since his last cholesterol check was about to ensue, that in a split second two families' lives would impact with a force that was devastating.

That two families' lives would be torn apart for ever.

She'd been playing tennis.

Trembling fingers pushed the key into the ignition as for the millionth time the day replayed itself in Isla's mind, the engine idling as she relived the awful events that had brought her to this point.

Sav had taken a long overdue morning off so she could take an extra tennis lesson. Wow the ladies with her fabulous serve at the comp that weekend!

Had she really been that shallow?

Isla could still see the ball thudding onto the line, hear the kookaburra's laughing in the treetops, feel the hot midmorning sun blazing on the back of her neck as the police car pulled up, a blue and white car out of place amongst the four-wheel-drives, a stir of interest rippling through the quiet suburban setting. She could feel her hand grip tighter on her racket as two officers got out, could still recall with total clarity the horrible shiver as someone pointed her out to them, taste the bile in her throat as they walked over, her legs dissolving as the news, however gently delivered, hit its mark.

That while she'd been hitting a bloody ball over a net, her husband lay trapped in the mangled wreckage of his car, that even now, as strong hands guided her to the waiting vehicle the emergency teams were trying to extricate him.

'Casey?'

The single question that no one would answer, the appalling wait in some hole of a room as the twins worked innocently on at school, pacing like a caged animal, desperate for answers but silently praying they wouldn't come.

She could still hear her scream as the doctor came in, feel her friend Louise's arms around her, even remembered feeling vaguely sorry for Louise that she'd had to arrive at that point, had to witness her friend literally collapse in a heap.

Checking her rear-view mirror as she pulled out of the driveway, Isla's eyes fixed for a second as they always did on the empty seat, almost willing Casey's cheeky smile to fill the

mirror, for that permanently chocolate-covered mouth to blow her a kiss just as he always did.
  Had.

CHAPTER THREE

'THIS is Isla Ramirez,' Jayne Davies, the charge nurse who had interviewed her, introduced a blushing Isla to the rest of the early shift. 'And before you ask, yes, she is related to the great man himself. This is, in fact, Sav's wife. No doubt some of you have already met her at some of Emergency's dos.'

The rather vague interest in the new nurse upped a notch then, and Isla blushed even more as not only did the gathered throng of nurses stare rather more closely but a couple of doctors, who were writing their notes at the nurses' station, looked up, clearly interested to see what the woman behind the great man looked like.

'Anyway, I'm sure Isla doesn't want her marital status to interfere with anything, so now we've got that bit of gossip out of the way, we'll let Hannah get started on the handover.'

It might not have been the most sensitive of introductions, but it was probably the most sensible.

Over and done with.

Yes, she was Sav's wife, but here she was just another nurse and that was exactly the way Isla wanted it.

The handover was fairly short, as the department was practically empty. Unlike the wards, where Isla had done the occasional shift over the last few years, an emergency room handover didn't involve sitting in an office with a mug of coffee, writing down every patient's ailment and treatment, because Emergency was a constantly evolving process so most of the handover was spent staring at the massive whiteboard which Hannah updated as she spoke, wiping out names or adding various treatments a doctor had ordered.

'The waiting room just has a few people in it,

mostly waiting for X-Ray to open. B-bay only has two patients. Mrs Ivy Dullard, 82 years of age, fell at home yesterday onto the coffee table and lay on the floor for approximately eight hours until her neighbour stopped by. She arrived in the department at 10 p.m. last night. A cantankerous old girl.' Hannah grinned. 'Thinks we're all out to steal her savings or rob her of her "last shred of dignity"—Mrs Dullard's words, not mine. Anyway, our main concern was her acute abdomen, but she's had a CT and that shows a small splenic haematoma, which the surgeons just want to observe.'

'In English for the students, please,' Jayne broke in.

'Sorry.' Hannah grinned again. 'Mrs Dullard has a small collection of blood on her spleen and possibly a small tear. There is a chance that could extend, which would mean she'd need surgery, but at this stage she'll be observed.'

'Thanks.' Jayne nodded. 'What else?'

'Her other major problem on arrival was a

shortened, externally rotated left leg. X-rays confirmed that she'd sustained a fractured neck of femur. She's nil by mouth on a six-hourly IV, we've given her morphine for pain, but she's still a bit agitated. We're hoping to get her up to Theatre soon....'

'How soon?' Jayne asked perceptively. 'She's already been here over nine hours now. She should be waiting on the ward, where she'd be more comfortable.'

'There isn't...' Hannah started, giving a rueful smile as the whole entourage chimed in with the final two words—'a bed'.

'Fair enough.' Jayne shook her head. 'But let's hope that Theatre rings down soon. You know how Sav feels about the emergency department being used as a holding bay. What are the Orthos doing now?'

'They've been operating through the night. We had two multiple injuries from a traffic accident last night. To be honest, I wouldn't be surprised if they wait for the next shift to perform Mrs Dullard's op. One other thing. She had a blood alcohol reading of nought point three when she came in, which isn't much, but given she'd been on the floor for quite some time, no doubt alcohol was a contributing factor to the fall. Still, she's fairly settled now, hopefully she'll be off to the ward soon.'

'Any relatives?' Isla asked automatically, and then snapped her mouth closed. But no one seemed remotely bothered by her assertion. In fact, Hannah gave a grateful nod.

'Good point. Sorry. Just the neighbour. She came in with Ivy and seemed very concerned, but Ivy made it very clear that we weren't to give her any information and sent her packing within the hour.

'Anyway, moving on. In Resus we've got Mr Jack Campbell, forty-six-year-old with central chest pain. No previous history. Ross Bowden, who's on for Cardiology, is looking at him now. He's had some morphine and Maxalon and for now at least he seems pretty comfortable—and that's your happy family.'

Isla stood uncomfortably as Jayne allocated

the staff to their various areas before turning her attention to the newest recruit.

'Feeling nervous?'

'Surprisingly, no.' Isla grinned. 'And considering how terrified I was this morning, it's hard to believe. Now I'm here, it feels as if I've never been away. There's still the age-old problem of finding beds and theatre space…'

'You did a fair bit of emergency work, didn't you?'

Isla nodded. 'I did my grad year in emergency, and then I did the advanced trauma course at the trauma centre. Not that I've put it to much use. I fell pregnant midway through it.'

'With the twins?' Jayne smiled. 'So you've been away from nursing for seven years.'

'A long seven years,' Isla admitted. 'I've been on the wards occasionally, but I haven't set foot in Emergency in all that time. I struggle to keep up with the television shows sometimes.'

'You'll be fine.' Jayne laughed. 'There's new

equipment, new drugs, new treatments and more politics, of course, but the patients are pretty much the same. You'll soon be back in the swing of things.'

'I hope so.'

'So what made you decide to come back?'

Isla gave a small shrug, consoling herself that for the most part she was talking the truth. She was hardly in a position to tell Jayne the real reason for her return. 'I've always loved emergency nursing, I've always missed it, and now the boys are at school it seemed like a good time.'

'It's a great time.' Jayne gave her a wide-eyed look. 'Believe me, an emergency nurse with your skills, however much they need updating, is more than welcome here. Now, how do you want to play this, Isla? A gentle start in the clinics or straight in the deep end out here with me?'

Isla hesitated, but only for a second. 'The deep end sounds good.'

'Great.' Jayne gave an appreciative nod.

'That's the best way, in my opinion. Kerry's in Resus today. If anything good comes in, you're more than welcome to go in and watch.'

Isla nodded, even managed a wry smile at Jayne's choice of words. 'Good' to an emergency nurse meant dramatic, gory or life-threatening—preferably all three.

'Now, a quick run-down of the doctors on this morning. Garth's the intern, new, eager, hasn't a clue, but doesn't mind being told. Heath's the registrar, thinks he knows everything.' Jayne rolled her eyes, and Isla did the same. 'In fairness, he's pretty on the ball, just doesn't like to be told…' Her voice petered out and Isla understood why as a rather good-looking blond man waltzed past and gave a brief wave.

'Morning, Heath!' Jayne called, and Isla's forehead furrowed as she tried to place his vaguely familiar face.

'He looks familiar. I must have seen him when I've called in to see Sav.'

'No doubt you've heard about him,' Jayne

added in a low whisper, and Isla gave a small nod. 'Still, it seems to have all settled down, but just bear history in mind, especially when Heath finds out that you're Sav's wife. Which brings me to the man himself. I'm sure you don't need to be told what a great guy he is— on the ball, easygoing, great to work with…'

'The real version, please, Jayne.' Isla grinned. 'I'm not his wife here, remember?'

'I'm giving you the real version,' Jayne replied, oblivious to the small frown starting to pucker Isla's brow. 'Of course he can let rip with that gorgeous Latin temper every once in a while if things aren't moving along as they should be, but he's such a honey, we all forgive him.

'Right, I'm going to ring Theatre and see what's happening. Maybe you could run a set of obs on Mrs Dullard and then I'll give you a guided tour.' As Isla made to go, Jayne called her back. 'Isla, if anything comes in, anything that you feel…'

'I'll be fine, Jayne,' Isla answered softly,

knowing what Jayne was referring to and grateful to her for raising the difficult subject. 'At least I hope I'll be fine. I suppose I won't really know till it happens.'

'Look, if you weren't Sav's wife, I wouldn't know about Casey, we wouldn't even be having this conversation. Maybe I shouldn't have raised it—'

'You were right to,' Isla broke in. 'I'm actually glad that you did.' She took a deep breath before going on. 'I've only done the occasional shift on the wards since I had children, but since Casey died I haven't worked a single shift. All I know is that emergency nursing is what I'm good at, what I'm trained to do, and if I don't come back to it now then I never will.'

'I'm here.' Jayne gave her a small smile. 'I know you've got Sav here and everything, but sometimes it's nice to unload on someone who's not so directly involved. So if something upsets you or you feel you're not coping just let me know.'

'Thanks.' Isla didn't look up, tears stinging her eyes.

'I've upset you,' Jayne said, but Isla shook her head.

'You haven't upset me at all. In fact, I'm grateful to you for bringing it up. I'm sure there will be times…' Her voice trailed off and Isla gave a small shake of her head. 'Let's just leave it there, but honestly, Jayne, I do appreciate you talking about this with me.'

It *did* feel as if she had never been away. OK, the blood-pressure cuffs were *all* automatic now, and glass thermometers seemed to have been relegated to museum pieces, but from her stints on the wards the equipment was for the most part familiar, and Isla felt her confidence increase as she accepted a few new patients from Triage and attempted to chat to Mrs Dullard while she recorded her half-hourly observations. A frail, emaciated-looking lady she might look, but there was a fire in her eyes that Isla instantly warmed to, a wary, proud defiance that Isla found endearing.

Isla liked elderly people, which should have been par for the course in nurses, but some, Isla thought, rushed past too quickly. It was their loss, she figured, because for the most part taking the time to listen, to draw from that knowledgeable pool was more reward than any pay packet, more satisfying than any neatly written notes at the end of the shift.

Especially when they were as old and as delightfully eccentric as Ivy Dullard! But Isla's gentle chatter evoked little response for the first hour or so. Ivy's beady eyes watched Isla's every move, but her little pink mouth stayed firmly closed.

She sat clutching her handbag firmly over her chest, the vivid smear of pink lipstick out of place with her rather wild grey hair. Each scrawny finger was decorated with a massive, loose ring and a yellow silk scarf was tied around her neck.

'How's your pain?' Isla asked.

'Fine. How's yours?' came the cheeky reply.

'I'm going to need to take your rings and scarf off, Mrs Dullard,' Isla said, her lips twitching as she smothered a smile. 'You can't wear them in Theatre.'

'They can be taped up—that's what they do on the television.'

Isla shook her head. 'A wedding band perhaps, but you've got rings on every finger! They'll be perfectly safe. I'll lock them up in the safe.'

'They're not real, you know!' Ivy declared, pulling them off one by one and popping them into her bag.

'They're not even worth ten cents.'

'They look nice.'

'Anything else?' Ivy demanded, and Isla gave an apologetic wince.

'I need the scarf as well.'

'You'll want me knickers next,' Mrs Dullard huffed, but as Isla nodded the old lady started to laugh. 'Lucky I didn't have any on, then, isn't it?

'Still, I'm not taking my lipstick off until I get

there, and I'm certainly not going to take my teeth out till the last moment. I've got some pride, and you can tell that to the anaesthetist!'

'Good for you.' Isla winked. 'I'll get you a container for your teeth—you can pop them out once you're up there.'

Those suspicious eyes finally softened slightly as she eyed Isla. 'How long do you think I'll be in here?' Ivy asked as Isla wrote down her obs. 'The doctor said they'd have me up out of bed by tomorrow!'

'If you're well enough,' Isla responded. 'A lot depends on your stomach injury, but on the whole it's been found that in the long term the quicker a patient is mobilized the fewer side effects are suffered. But it will all be done gently. The physio will be the one who gets you up and we won't expect you to be racing around the ward.'

'That wasn't what I asked—when will I get out?' Pursing her lips, Ivy ran her hand again through her shock of grey hair, and Isla noticed it was anything but steady, her slightly jerky movements increasing.

'We'll know a lot more when you've been to Theatre, Mrs Dullard. Is there anything troubling you?'

'Apart from a broken hip, you mean?'

Smiling inwardly at the old lady's sharp tongue, Isla pushed on.

'Yes, apart from your broken hip, Mrs Dullard.'

'I've got a cat, Treacle.' Rummaging through her bag, she pulled out her purse and held out a photo, but Isla's eyes were drawn more to the contents inside her bag, though she didn't let on straightaway.

'She's gorgeous.'

'It's a he,' Mrs Dullard corrected. 'And he's twenty years old, which is about my age in cat years. We've never been apart.'

'Is there someone who could feed him?' Isla asked, which only served to incense the old lady.

'Oh, wouldn't Amy just love that?'

'Amy's the neighbour who called the ambulance?' Isla checked.

'Busybody,' Mrs Dullard sniffed.

'Sometimes even busybodies serve their purpose. If she hadn't come around when she did, you could still be lying on the floor.'

'Perhaps, but now she's got my front door key, and no doubt she's poking around in all my things as we speak.'

'Do you want me to arrange a social worker to come and talk to you?' As Ivy opened her mouth to argue, Isla carried on talking. 'She could collect your key from the neighbour, if that's what you want, and she can help you work out what to do with Treacle while you're in here.

'Now…' Keeping her voice deliberately light, Isla moved on to a rather more difficult subject. 'Do you have any valuables that need to be locked in the safe?'

'I've done that,' Ivy snapped. 'They've already taken my money out of my purse and my bus pass.'

'Good.' Isla's eyes drifted pointedly to the open bag. 'Mrs Dullard, you know that you're nil by mouth?' When the old lady didn't answer, Isla pushed on. 'That means you can't have anything at all to eat or drink.'

'I'm not stupid.'

'No,' Isla said slowly, 'but you've had a lot of powerful drugs that can make you a little bit confused. Now, on a ward, we generally clear the patient's locker and table of any food or drink…'

'I haven't got anything.'

'You've got a half bottle of vodka in your bag, Mrs Dullard,' Isla said evenly. 'And as I've said, it's very easy to forget that you're nil by mouth sometimes.'

'Do you really think I'm likely to have a drink of vodka at eight in the morning?'

'I don't know,' Isla admitted. 'But if you did, it could have some very serious consequences. It's imperative that your stomach is empty for the anaesthetic. I'd feel a lot happier if you let

me put the drink along with your other belong-
ings.'

'It might get taken.'

'Well, I can lock it up in the safe with your
valuables, then.'

For a second the old lady bristled and Isla
braced herself for a rather curt few words, but
surprisingly she fished in her bag and handed
over the bottle with
out more protest.

'I suppose you think I've got a problem.'

'I didn't say that…'

'*I didn't say that,*' Ivy mimicked. 'Standing
there all haughty and judging me.'

'Nobody's judging you, Mrs Dullard. If it
was a can of cola in your bag, I'd have asked
the same thing. Now, I'll go and lock this up
in the safe for you and then I'll come back and
see how you're doing.'

'Please, don't.' Gripping Isla's hand, the elderly lady struggled to sit up, wincing as the
pain gripped her. 'Please, don't leave me.'

'Mrs Dullard—'

'Ivy.'

'Ivy,' Isla soothed. 'Have you got more pain?'

'I just want to know where you've put Treacle. I just want someone to come and tell me what's happening.' Tears started then, but angry, frustrated tears. She let go of Isla's hand and rattled the side of the hospital gurney in a futile attempt to get down.

'Mrs Dullard—Ivy—you need to stay still. You need to lie back and calm down and tell me what's wrong.' Pushing the button on the automatic blood-pressure machine, Isla tried to calm the elderly woman as Heath came over with Jayne.

'What's the problem?'

'Eighty-two-year-old…' Jayne started, then paused, nodding for Isla to carry on. 'I'll leave you to it. Call if you need a hand.'

Alone, Isla faced her first handover.

'Ivy Dullard, fell at home last night and sustained fractured neck of femur and a splenic haematoma. She's waiting to go to Theatre for a dynamic hip screw, but has just become increasingly agitated and confused. Her obs have been stable, but her blood pressure's dropped slightly to 110 over 60 and her pulse is now 100, up from 80.'

'Any head injury?' Heath asked.

'None noted.'

'What are they doing about her spleen?' Heath asked, pulling back the blanket and probing Ivy's abdomen, much to her indignation.

'The surgeons have reviewed the CT and want to treat it conservatively at this stage. Do you want me to page them for a review?'

'What's with the vodka?' Heath asked, ignoring Isla's question and nodding to the bottle she was holding.

'She had a blood alcohol of nought point three on arrival. I found this in her bag. I was just about to lock it up.'

Heath gave a knowing nod and scribbled on the casualty card. 'OK, give her 5 milligrams of diazepam and I'll give the orthos and anaesthetist a call. She'll need to be reviewed again before she goes to the Theatre.'

'Do you want me to page the surgeons?' Isla asked as he walked off, holding her breath as Heath turned on his heel and faced her. 'I mean, it could be her abdomen…' Isla swallowed hard. Her first patient, her first day and here she was questioning a registrar.

It really was just like old times.

'Her blood pressure's down, her heart rate's up, she's confused…'

'Which are the symptoms of alcohol withdrawal,' Heath said tartly. 'I've just examined her abdomen and there's no increased tenderness.'

'But she's had morphine,' Isla pointed out. Maybe it wasn't just like old times, maybe things had changed after all, because at twenty-three years of age she'd have been blushing to her roots and mentally berating herself for causing a scene. But seven years on and it was a tougher, more confident woman that faced this rather difficult situation, and she didn't even waver as Jayne came over to find out what was going on. 'The fact Mrs Dullard's had morphine means she isn't going to be feeling pain.'

'Are you questioning my judgment, Sister?'

Isla took a deep breath, wondering how best to play this, deciding that Heath's rather inflamed ego wouldn't take the response that was on the tip of her tongue. 'I'm just concerned that Mrs Dullard has gone downhill so quickly…'

'Since you tried to take away her alcohol…'

'Morning!'

She had sensed Sav before she had heard him, had smelt the delicious tangy aftershave that had filled her nostrils this morning, heard the confident footsteps as they approached. But what wasn't familiar, what was surprisingly different, was the light-heartedness in his voice, the cheery note to the single word.

'A bit early in the career comeback to be hitting the bottle, Isla.' Sav grinned and Isla clutched the vodka, staring utterly bemused at the man smiling back at her. A man she hadn't seen in fourteen months, the haughty yet smiling face of the man that she used to know.

'What's going on?'

'Nothing,' Heath snarled.

'Nothing?' Sav checked, clearly picking up on the tension. 'It doesn't sound like nothing.'

'I asked the new nurse to get some Valium that I prescribed for a patient.'

'And?' Sav's eyes swung between the two.

'I'm still waiting.'

There was the longest pause, which Isla finally filled. 'I'm concerned that perhaps I didn't give Dr Jameson a relevant enough handover. I have an elderly lady with a fractured neck of femur and abdominal injuries—'

'Who has alcohol withdrawal,' Heath snapped. 'Now, are you going to get the drug I ordered or not, Sister?'

'*I'll* get the Valium.' Jayne stepped in. 'Isla, you stay with Mrs Dullard. Here, give me the vodka. I'll lock it up for you.'

Only Sav would have registered the angry set

of Isla's lips, the glint in her eye as she handed over the bottle without a word. Clearly, in his eyes at least, she was annoyed that Jayne had overridden her in an effort to keep the peace.

'I'll come in and have a look,' Sav said as Isla slipped back into the cubicle.

'Fiery little thing, isn't she?' Heath smirked as the two men were left alone. 'I'll guarantee there's a flash of red under that gorgeous blonde hair.'

'Can we get back to discussing the patient?' Sav snapped, but Heath wasn't listening.

'Nice figure, too,' he mused. 'You know, I can't help thinking I've seen her before…'

'You have,' Sav said in a clipped voice, fixing Heath with a warning glare. 'At last year's Christmas party. Isla's my wife.'

Heath didn't even blush, just gave a vaguely apologetic grin, the smile only wiped off his face when Isla's summons came from inside the cubicle, the loud but controlled call for assistance which had everyone suddenly running.

'Can I have some help in here? *Now!*'

CHAPTER FOUR

FOR a second Isla froze.

Less than a second, probably.

Pulling back the curtain, seeing Ivy lying pale and unresponsive on the trolley, her vibrant pink mouth horribly slack now, Isla assessed the scene, processed a hundred thoughts almost immediately.

Reflexes she had worried might not know how to respond snapped to attention as she crossed the short distance to the gurney, calling her patient's name and attempting to rouse her while simultaneously lowering the head of the gurney so her patient lay flat.

'Can I have…?' Isla's voice was barely a croak and the background noise of the hospital was too loud for her colleagues to hear her anxious plea, but the emergency bell was on the other side. Clearing her throat, Isla gave another shout as she pulled on gloves and checked Ivy's airway, noting it was patent. She watched the rapid but shallow rise and fall of Ivy's chest as her own fingers probed the flickering pulse in Ivy's neck, while with her free hand she punched the button on the blood-pressure cuff.

'What have we got?'

Sav was beside her, taking control in an instant, grabbing the oxygen mask from Isla and placing it over Ivy's mouth as she turned the oxygen on to ten litres.

'I found her collapsed and unresponsive, her resps are rapid and shallow, pulse over a hundred and weak...'

'Blood pressure?'

On cue the monitor delivered its reading. 'Eighty on forty. It was a hundred on sixty ten minutes ago.'

'OK. Open the IV full bore.'

'I have.'

'Let's get her over to Resus. Get some O-negative blood ready...'

'She's already been cross-matched.' Isla's voice was slightly breathless as she kicked off the brakes and pushed the gurney over the polished tiles, Heath running ahead to wait for them in Resus.

'Right, ring the lab, tell Len, the porter, to run up and fetch two units and page the surgeons...'

'Done!' Jayne was back, with the Valium in the kidney dish. She gave Isla a tiny wink that, frankly, Isla was too busy to interpret.

'Good,' Sav barked, skidding the trolley into Resus and swinging it around so that the head of the trolley was against the wall. 'Page Theatre as well and let them know to expect her soon.' Picking up the wall phone, Isla punched in the number for the switchboard, grateful it was written in red on the telephone, and told the operator the urgent pages she wanted put out.

Then it hit her.

Hit her in a way she'd never anticipated when she'd first considered coming back, and she realized that she hadn't been lying at all when she'd spoken to Jayne that morning.

Watching as the crash cart was opened, Kerry wheeling over the ultrasound machine, the well-polished wheels of Emergency rolling into action, Isla realized there and then how much she'd missed this.

Missed this.

That pit-of-the-stomach flutter of nerves kicking in as the adrenaline started flowing, the frantic race against the large ticking stopwatch mounted on the wall to save a life. And it was, for Isla, like watching a much-loved movie, one you hadn't seen for ages, had somehow forgotten the frantic twists that made you gasp, the drama, the tension that had you on the edge of your seat.

'Theatre's standing by.' Isla spoke over the low urgent tones as the surgeons flew in. She took the blood from a breathless Len and, almost as naturally as breathing, picked up Ivy's limp hand and proceeded to check the details on her name band against the precious life force she held in her other hand.

'We'll need the blood warmer,' Jayne called, but Kerry was already setting it up, a far more sophisticated model than Isla was used to.

Isla focused for now on what she knew, connecting the giving set to the bag of blood and feeding the precious fluid down the long line that would coil inside the machine and warm the refrigerated blood to body temperature, a necessary requisite when rapid infusion was needed.

'I need that blood,' Sav called, as he inserted another wide-bore IV, his hand absolutely steady as Isla handed the end of the giving set over while Kerry punched the buttons, telling Isla what she was doing as she did so.

'Punch in the desired temp—it's generally already set—then snap the lever into place and press the go button. I've set it at a stat rate.'

'And that's it?' Isla asked, impressed, recalling the rather large trays of water they had filled just a few short years ago to warm the blood as it coiled through the giving set.

'That's it.' Kerry nodded.

'Was this Valium given?' The astute eyes of the anaesthetist scanned Ivy's notes as he pulled up drugs and laid them by the head of the trolley for easy access. Even though she was still breathing, her respiratory effort wasn't allowing for adequate oxygenation and everyone present knew it was only a matter of time before she stopped breathing or went into cardiac arrest unless a full and effective resuscitation with fluids commenced.

'Thankfully, no.' Sav's voice was bland but the withering stare he shot Heath could have melted ice at a hundred paces. '*We* initially thought her confusion was because she was suffering from alcohol withdrawal.'

'That was my call,' Heath volunteered, and Isla's rather low opinion of Heath nudged up a small fraction. Everyone made mistakes, and in fairness Heath hadn't technically made one, just jumped the gun a touch. 'Given her blood alcohol reading on arrival and the fact the sister had just found a bottle of vodka in her bag, I wrongly assumed that was what her problem was.'

'You're not necessarily wrong.' The surgeon looked up from where he was examining Ivy's abdomen. 'Her agitation may well have been a contributory factor in her laceration extending, but right now her main problem is the fact she's bleeding out. Let's get her straight up to Theatre.'

And that was it.

Or almost.

'Ivy?' Leaning over the elderly lady, Isla called her name. Holding the pale hand, Isla squeezed it tightly, noting with quiet relief that the pressure was returned. Ivy's pale eyelashes flickered slightly, the blood and oxygen and aggressive resuscitation clearly taking effect. 'You're going to be OK.'

For a second Isla struggled with what to say, how much Ivy would comprehend. Her signature on a consent form was out of the question when she couldn't even open her eyes. 'We're taking you to Theatre now and afterwards you'll be on a ward. We're looking after you.'

Almost imperceptibly under the green oxygen mask Ivy's lips moved, the vivid smear of lipstick out of place in her exsanguinated face.

'We need to move her,' Sav ordered. It could have been anyone speaking and Isla's response would have been the same.

'Hold on!' Putting up her hand as the trolley started to move, Isla's irritation was evident. Yes, it was urgent, yes, Ivy's injuries were life-threatening, but she was an eighty-two-year-old woman and with the best will in the world, with the best modern medicine had to offer, there was a fair chance she wouldn't make it. Ivy deserved a chance to speak if at all possible. 'Ivy, did you want to say something?'

A tiny nod was her only answer and to the surgeon's obvious irritation Isla lifted the mask and waited as Ivy ran a dry tongue over her lips, before finally mouthing a single word.

'Amy.'

'Amy?' Isla checked. 'Your neighbour, Amy? Don't worry, Ivy…'

'Si—' Again Ivy struggled to speak. 'My sister.'

Isla gave a small, gentle laugh, squeezed the old lady's hand a little harder. 'She's not a busybody, then, Ivy, she loves you. I'll tell her what's happening. You just concentrate on getting better.'

'Tell her I love her, too.'

And she was gone.

Resus doors sliding open, a couple of bumps as Ivy's IV pole hit the doorframe, the surgeons running on ahead to scrub as Kerry and the porter started the mercy dash up to Theatre and Sav paged the orthos to let them know what had taken place. Isla stood there for a moment, in the empty space where Ivy's gurney had been. Resus was noticeably quiet now, the chaos of the last fifteen minutes evident, half-opened packs discarded, wrappings littering the floor. Isla started the task of cleaning up and restocking.

'Welcome back!' Jayne gave her a rueful smile. 'About before…'

'It's fine.' Isla shook her head. 'Heath's the doctor.'

'It has nothing to do with that,' Jayne replied. 'I paged the surgeons *while* I fetched the Valium. As Sav said, there probably was an element of alcohol withdrawal, but at the same time I knew you weren't likely to make a fuss unnecessarily, especially on your first day.'

'Don't believe it for a minute.' Sav's heavily accented voice made both women jump, but for different reasons. Jayne, having been unaware of his presence, swung around, while Isla blinked in surprise as the Sav of old seemed to materialize before her eyes, his seductive mouth curving into a lazy smile, his easy chatter, relaxed mannerisms such a teasing glimpse of the man who had turned her world around all those years ago. 'I met Isla on her first day as a grad nurse and, believe me, there was nothing submissive about her. I believe the first words we exchanged were in the heat of a row.'

For a beat of a second Isla stared dumbly at him, stunned, completely stunned at the change in him, almost as if the agony of the past fourteen months had never happened, as if the pain that had brought them to this point was an awful figment of her imagination. The delicious, effusive charismatic man she had mourned for so long was suddenly back, but the welcome in her heart faded almost as quickly as it had started. Seeing Jayne smiling back at her, clearly completely at ease with this side of Sav, had Isla's mind whirring, tiny flames of anger licking the edges of her confusion.

'Isn't that right, Isla?' Sav prompted, but still she stood there, staring utterly dumbfounded at him. What she had expected on her return to work Isla truly hadn't known—scathing superiority, vague irritation, cold indifference even, but not this.

Never this.

'Well, good for Isla,' Jayne said instead, oblivious to the undercurrents. 'Emergency can always use a nurse with a bit of spark. I'd better get rid of this Valium.' Picking up the kidney dish Jayne moved off.

'I'll come with you and sign for it,' Isla offered, but Jayne waved away her offer.

'I'll be fine. Can I leave you to finish the clean-up and keep an eye on Mr Campbell? Kerry will help when she gets back, but it's a good way to find your way around Resus and work out where everything's kept for yourself.'

'Fine.' Isla nodded. 'Fine,' she said again as Jayne breezed off, leaving her facing Sav as if for the first time, the silence deafening until finally Isla broke it.

'What was that, Sav?'

'What?'

'That!' angry eyes flashed at him, angry, bewildered eyes as she struggled to hold it together, a shaking hand running over her forehead. She shook her head to clear her thoughts, knowing this was neither the time nor place for a private discussion, but they had been married too long for Sav to misinterpret her single word, the shorthand language couples reverted to easily translated as his mouth set in the familiar grim line. Black eyes stared back at her and they both simultaneously moved a few steps out of earshot of the remaining patient.

'Are you accusing me of flirting?'

'Flirting!' Isla gave an incredulous snort. 'You think I'm worried you were flirting?'

'I would hope not.' Finally he looked at her. 'Because the last woman I flirted with, Isla, was you.'

'I know.' Swallowing hard, she felt an angry blush spread over her cheeks.

'And if every time I have a laugh or joke with one of the staff, it is going to evoke this type of response, it would seem my doubts about us working alongside each other were merited after all.'

Somehow the conversation had turned. With one stroke he had tipped it into the dangerous territory of the bedroom, where Sav always won, but Isla stood firm, refusing to allow him to relegate this to the rantings of a jealous wife.

'I just don't understand how come you're so different here.' Her voice was low and urgent. 'How you're suddenly so nice, so easygoing, everyone's best friend.'

'Because, Isla,' Sav replied crisply, 'I'm at work.' And stalking off, he left her reeling in confusion.

Resus had long since been cleaned, the department that had started nearly empty was full now, and Isla had made more trips to X-Ray and the wards than she cared to remember before she faced him again.

But he was everywhere.

'Sav?'

His name was the single word on everyone's lips, the one man they could all turn to for advice, the absolute lynchpin of the department, and Isla watched from a relative distance and witnessed at first-hand the demands that were placed on him over and over again, from a fretful parent refusing an anaesthetic for their child to an irate nursing coordinator insisting there were no beds, yet somehow he managed to deal with each and every request, somehow he managed to literally be in three places at once, kind but stern, authoritative yet sympathetic.

The man she had fallen in love with.

'Sister Ramirez?' An exceptionally well-groomed elderly woman, teetering towards her in a smart tweed suit and high heels, dragged Isla out of her introspection as she remade a gurney after taking yet another patient to a ward. 'The receptionist told me I should speak to you. My name is Amy Baker.'

'Ivy's sister.' Isla smiled, shaking the woman's hand. 'I'll just let the consultant know that you're here and then see if there's somewhere more private where we can talk.'

'Ivy's not…?' Amy started, and Isla quickly shook her head.

'Ivy's in Theatre,' Isla responded calmly but firmly. 'She took a turn for the worse, that's why I contacted you.'

'I was just at the shops, buying her some toiletries and a couple of nightdresses.' She waved a few carrier bags as Isla darted over to the nurses' station where Sav stood juggling a phone call, the intern and the casualty card he was writing on.

'Sav.' Even Isla managed a wry smile as she joined in the chime of people vying for his attention. 'I've got Ivy Dullard's sister here. I left a message on her answering-machine, asking her to come up.'

'What does she know?' Sav asked, straight to the point and barely looking up as he wrote on the back of a casualty card and barked a few orders down the
telephone.

'Just that Ivy's in Theatre.'

'OK.' His eyes scanned the whiteboard and, picking up a marker, he scribbled Ivy's name on one of the free boxes and added Amy's. 'Put her in interview room two, tell her…' He gave a small shrug. 'You know the drill, Isla. I'll be along soon.'

'Fine.' Isla stood there for a second as Sav frowned down at her.

'You've spoken to relatives before, Isla,' Sav pointed out.

'Many times.' Isla bristled. 'I just don't happen to know where interview room two is.'

It was Sav giving a wry smile now. 'Sorry.' He looked almost sheepish. 'I guess from the way you've been this morning, I somehow expected you to know. It's over there.' He pointed and as Isla made to go he pulled her back, well, not pulled exactly but his fingers brushed her polo shirt, his hands closing loosely around her upper arm. Isla swallowed hard, brutally aware of the contact, as Sav spoke in lower tones. 'That was a compliment, by the way.'

'Was it?'

Bewildered eyes turned to his.

'You're good at this, Isla.' He stared down at her, really stared, and it wasn't Sav the consultant, wasn't Sav the doctor, but Sav the man looking into her eyes now. 'Maybe you were right to come back after all.'

She'd loved to have dwelt on it, would have loved to roll his words over and over in her mind, but Amy was waiting and, taking the lead, Isla led her to the small interview room.

'First of all,' Isla explained as she looked around the room with the same unfamiliar eyes as Amy, 'this is my first day here, so I'm not very well versed on all the doctors' names, or where the relatives' toilets are....'

'That's fine.' Amy smiled, obviously grateful for Isla's honesty. She took a seat where Isla gestured. 'You said on the telephone that Ivy had been taken to Theatre.'

'That's right.' Isla nodded. 'What do you know about Ivy's injuries?'

'That she's broken her hip,' Amy ventured. 'And that she has a small tear on her...' Her face crinkled in confusion.

'On her spleen,' Isla said, and Amy nodded.

'That's right, although the surgeons said that it didn't need an operation, that they were just going to observe it. That's pretty much all I know. Soon after that Ivy got cross with me and told me to leave.'

'When I came on this morning,' Isla started, choosing her words carefully, not wanting to unduly alarm Amy but not wanting either to underplay the severity of Ivy's condition, 'Ivy was quite comfortable, her observations were stable and she was waiting to go to Theatre for a hip repair. However, she became extremely confused and agitated and it soon became apparent that she was unwell. It would appear that the injury on her spleen had extended, which required her to be taken urgently to surgery. That's where she is now.'

Isla let her words sink in, looking up quietly as the door opened and Sav came in.

'This is Sav, he's the emergency consultant,' Isla introduced them, gently omitting his surname to avoid Amy losing track of the conversation. 'I was just explaining to Mrs Baker how Ivy deteriorated fairly rapidly this morning and that at this stage we believe it was due to the wound on her spleen extending.'

Sav gave a grateful nod and sat down.

'Is she going to die, Doctor?' Amy's voice had a pained dignity behind it, her slender body bolt upright as she addressed Sav, an utter contrast to her feisty sister. But there were similarities. The make-up on Amy Baker was beautifully applied but, like Ivy's, there was nothing subtle about it, and they both clearly shared a passion for loud jewellery, though something told Isla that the many rings adorning Amy's fingers were real.

'I cannot say.' Sav's accent was thick, but his words were very clear. 'Your sister is elderly and also, from what I have seen of her, she appears rather weak and undernourished.'

'She doesn't eat,' Amy confirmed. 'I take her a meal every night but it ends up in the bin.'

'Any operation has its risks, but for someone in your sister's condition the risks will be greater. I have to say, though, Mrs Baker, that initially we were unsure as to the reason for your sister's agitation.'

'She doesn't need a reason.' Amy gave a

pained smile. 'Ivy's very good at getting agitated.'

'She drinks?' Sav checked, and Isla could only admire his directness.

'A lot,' Amy admitted. 'Since she lost her husband.'

'Did he die recently?' Sav asked, but Amy shook her head.

'Twenty years ago. I've tried to help her, I've tried over and over to get her to stop, but she tells me that I'm just interfering, to leave her alone. I don't know what else I can do.'

'Until Ivy admits she has a problem, there's really not a lot that you can do,' Sav said gently, 'except be there for her, which you clearly have been.'

'Ivy doesn't even like that. She's never really liked me. Since we were little Ivy's always been jealous of me, because I'm younger and prettier than her.' She gave a low laugh. 'Can you believe I'm seventy-five years old and saying that?'

'That's families for you.' Sav smiled gently.

'We've always fought. She couldn't have children, so I tried to keep her close to mine, not to
share them with her exactly, but I hoped she'd
be a special aunt, that she'd be close to them,
but instead of doting on mine, she moaned that
they were too noisy, too naughty. You know
what children are like…' Amy was rambling
now and they both let her, knowing that sometimes idle talk was needed when bad news was
processed. 'Now, when the grandchildren come
over, she gets even crosser, says that they're out
of control and disturbing her peace when
they're just being children. Do you have children, Doctor?'

'I have twin boys,' Sav said, and Amy gave a
trembling smile.

'Then you know what it's like.' Her eyes
turned to Isla, who sat there, face paling, tears
pricking her eyes at Sav's cruel dismissal, her
mouth as dry as sand. 'What about you, Sister?
How many have you had?'

Isla could feel Sav's discomfort, feel in that
tiny beat of time the abyss between them

widen. 'Three,' Isla said softly, somehow finding her voice, somehow managing to hold it all in. 'I've had three.'

'Ivy sounds very lonely,' Sav ventured, clearing his throat and shifting the conversation. 'Isla here found some vodka in her bag which she took from her—with Ivy's consent, of course—but afterwards Ivy became very upset. We assumed, wrongly as it turned out, that it was alcohol withdrawal that was causing her confusion, but it became apparent very quickly that there was a physical reason for her confusion. Her blood pressure dropped very suddenly, so we moved her over to Resus and treated her aggressively, and by the time she went to Theatre she was responsive.'

'Did she say anything?' Amy asked, tears sparkling in her lavishly made-up eyes.

'She asked me to let you know,' Isla said, glad, so glad that whatever the outcome Amy would have something to cling to, 'that she loved you.'

'I don't think so.' A tear slid down Amy's

face and her strained smile was almost patronizing. 'It's very sweet of you to try—'

'Isla isn't trying to make you feel better here, Mrs Baker. Our job is to deliver the facts to you, which hopefully we have,' Sav said firmly but kindly.

Isla watched with her breath bursting in her lungs as he put out a hand and squeezed the woman's shoulders, imparting comfort so easily, instinctively knowing what this stranger needed. Inexplicably Isla was jealous—jealous that even though it was merited, even though it was absolutely the right thing to do, Sav could somehow reach out, could comfort a stranger in their darkest of moments, yet, for whatever reason, he simply couldn't do it for her.

'I have to get back out to the department now, Mrs Baker,' Sav said, standing up, 'but as soon as we hear from Theatre we will let you know.'

'He's very nice,' Amy said after Sav had left and Isla sat staring at her hands, wrestling with her emotions. Sav's lingering scent still filled the room, but every word Amy uttered merely twisted the knife further into Isla's heart. 'Very honest and open,' Amy continued. 'I admire that in a man.'

CHAPTER FIVE

JAYNE had told her to go and take her lunch-break, but even a well earned forty-five minutes, sitting with her feet up, paled into insignificance as Sav stalked passed the staff-room and headed for his office, laughing over his shoulder at something a passing colleague had said, incensing Isla so much that with barely a thought she marched down the corridor behind him, knocking once on his office door and not waiting for a reply before pushing it open.

'How dare you dismiss him?'

'This isn't the place, Isla.' Sav barely even bothered to look up as she exploded into his office, slamming the door behind her, two spots of colour flaming on her cheeks, angry tears glistening in her eyes. His voice had a warning ring to it which Isla chose to ignore.

'Oh, I'd say this is exactly the place, Sav. This is probably the only place where I'm actually going to get more than a sentence out of you. How dare you just dismiss Casey?'

'Did you want me to tell her, Isla?' There was a challenge in his voice that unnerved her, pushing her an inch off her high moral ground as Sav stared coldly at her. 'Did you want me to sit in the interview room and tell a virtual stranger who already had enough on her mind that fourteen months ago yesterday I lost my son?'

'No…' Her mind spun like a merry-go-round, her lips chasing a response that simply wouldn't come, and like a petulant child almost, Isla stamped her foot in frustration, appalled that he couldn't see it, devastated that Sav quite simply couldn't see the problem.

'You can do it when your mum rings, or a neighbour drops by, you can do it for the kids, hell, you can do it for a stranger in the street, but you still can't do it for me.'

'Do what exactly?' His voice was supremely even, as if she were some sort of lunatic he had to pacify until Security arrived.

'Be nice.' She gave an exasperated shrug. 'Your mum rings and you light up…'

'I do the same for your parents,' Sav pointed out. 'And as for my mother, she's in Spain, Isla. She's on the other side of the world, worried sick about us all. What do you want me to do, cry into the telephone and make her load just that bit heavier? Or maybe I should answer the door to your parents and tell them just how I'm feeling!'

'Tell *me*, then,' Isla begged. 'Tell me how you're feeling, Sav.'

'OK, then.' He stared back at her, black eyes flashing, his mouth in a grim line, that gorgeous olive complexion tinged with grey, and for a tiny second she thought he was going to do it, was going to finally open up and let her in, but instead he gave a tight shrug.

'Hungry.' He glanced at his watch. 'At this moment I'm feeling hungry, so I'm going to the canteen.'

'Sav, please.' She was crying now, but not in weakness. Instead, angry tears of utter exasperation were coursing down her cheeks as she faced this impossible, difficult man. 'I can't do this any more!'

'Can't do what?' he snapped. 'What exactly is your problem here, Isla?'

'You are!' Isla rasped, her fists clenched in rage. 'For twelve months you've shut me out, for twelve months you've barely spoken to me, and I've tried to understand, tried to accept that it's your way of coping, and then I come in here and you're outgoing, laughing, being nice…'

'I'm paid to be nice, Isla.' Stapling a few papers together, he finally deigned to look at her. 'Did you expect to find me hiding in my office with my head in my hands?'

'Of course not.'

'This department sees more than one hundred thousand new arrivals a year.'

'I don't need some impromptu audit, Sav—'

'Perhaps you do,' he said promptly. 'Perhaps, Isla, you need to understand that I am a consultant, that I have to, *have* to,' he reiterated, 'hold my staff together, be accountable, foster a team spirit, and as much as I'd like to shut the door on the lot of them I can't.' His voice was low but there was an urgency behind it and Isla's eyes widened as he continued. 'You're very good at blaming me for all of this, you're very good at pointing out my inadequacies over the last twelve months, very good at telling me that I don't show enough emotion—but our son died *fourteen* months ago, Isla.' He watched her paling face, watched as her head started to slowly shake, her lips quivering as he mercilessly continued. '*Fourteen* months ago,' Sav repeated slowly. 'So why don't we fill in the gaps? Let's talk about the first two months after he died, shall we?'

'No!' Suddenly the ball she had started to roll

seemed to be gaining in momentum, but it was hurtling in the wrong direction and Isla floundered to control it. 'Not here.'

'Why not?' Sav stared directly at her. 'I thought talking was what you wanted. I can assure you no one can hear or will come in.'

'No!' she said again, putting her hands up to her ears, but Sav was relentless in his pursuit.

'For those two months I held it together, Isla. I alone held the family together,' he repeated. 'For those two months, despite my surgery, despite the fact that three weeks after the funeral I had to go back and work full-time in a new role as a consultant, I was the one making the meals, bathing and feeding the twins and arranging transport to take them to and from school, practically spoon-feeding you while you lay in bed. Didn't it dawn on you that I might have wanted the world to stop for a while? Didn't you ever think I might have needed to shut the door on everyone and disappear? But I couldn't. I had a wife practically incoherent with grief, two little boys whose world had been torn apart and, like it or not, as irrelevant as it might have seemed at the time, a mortgage to pay. One of us had to be strong, and I expected it to be me, I wanted it to be me. But for those two months I held it in, for those two months I was the one comforting you, the twins and our families, and now suddenly, because you're ready to talk, ready to move on, I have to be, too.'

'It isn't suddenly,' Isla refuted, but the certainty had left her voice now. Sav's argument was unexpectedly persuasive and she struggled to retrieve the clarity of earlier, the angry wind that had swept her into his office, her tear-filled eyes beseeching him to understand. 'I know I wasn't there for you, I know those months must have been hell...'

'It's all been hell,' Sav corrected.

'My son had died...' Isla rasped, but Sav sat unmoved.

'So had mine.' He stared back at her and suddenly everything swirled into focus, her whole perspective on that awful, vile time shifting that immovable inch. She finally witnessed Sav's take on things, comprehending, perhaps for the first time, that she wasn't entirely blameless in all this. That the demise of their marriage wasn't squarely Sav's fault.

It was a sobering thought indeed.

'So had mine,' Sav said again, picking up the telephone that had rung unnoticed for a couple of moments. 'I'll be there in a moment. Thanks for letting me know,' he said into the phone.

'Sav.' Pale, trembling, she caught the sleeve of his jacket as he brushed past, but when he turned to face her, Isla truly didn't know what to say. In that single moment everything, *everything* had changed.

'We're needed out there.'

CHAPTER SIX

'COME ON, Isla.' Jayne was sipping on a coffee, as she juggled the off-duty roster. 'It will be a great evening, a real chance for you to get to know everyone.'

'I really can't.' Shaking her head, Isla finished up the notes she was writing, painfully aware that Sav was sitting next to her. Yesterday's explosive revelation was still hanging in the air, unexplored thanks to Sav being called into the hospital last night. And despite her earlier needed for laying it all out in the open, Isla was grateful for the small reprieve. She felt as if she'd got out of bed for the first time after a horrendous dose of flu, her legs impossibly shaky, the world strangely unfamiliar, her mind slowly, painfully coming to terms with her own behaviour. The two months after Casey's death had been a swirling fog of pain she had never revisited, something she had pushed aside in the name of self-preservation, but clearly it had to be faced.

'Come on,' Jayne pushed. 'Sav's not on call, the two of you will have a ball. Every month the emergency staff get together, all of us, not just the doctors and nurses, but the domestic and admin staff as well. Some of the paramedics come, too, if they can make it. It's great to meet up away from work. I swear it keeps us all sane.'

'Or suitably insane.' Sav grinned. 'You'd have to be to work here.'

'Exactly.' Jayne laughed. 'Come on, Isla, we're going Middle Eastern tomorrow night. There's a great restaurant at the Docklands everyone wants to try.'

'Let's go!' Sav looked up from his notes and Isla blinked in surprise at his response.

'But what if you get called in?' Isla answered, her mind flailing, suddenly appalled at the prospect of a night out, their first night out since, since…

Forcibly she pushed that thought away, thinking up an excuse with a slightly triumphant glint in her eye. 'Martin's still away for another fortnight. We can go next month.'

'I won't drink.' Sav gave an easy shrug. 'Jordan's the registrar on this Saturday night and he's more than capable of running the show, but if he needs me to come in for anything he can call me at the restaurant. Why don't you ask your parents if they can babysit?' He flashed that dazzling smile at Jayne as he fished in his wallet for a fifty-dollar note. 'Here's our deposit. Put us both down.' Ignoring Isla's wide-eyed look of annoyance, aimed solely at him, that dazzling smile widened a good inch, halting her argument as the doors slid open and the bright green overalls of the paramedics came into view. 'Looks like you've got a new patient, Sister.'

Isla wasn't sure who was blushing more, the

cheery paramedic who was handing over the latest arrival or herself.

'Jamie Chappell, eight years old, had an asthma attack at school. This is his teacher, Miss Symons. The parents know and are on their way in.'

'Thank you.' Isla smiled, unable to look the paramedic or his partner in the eye, then forcing herself to do so, to tackle yet another difficult situation head-on and acknowledge that she recognized them, that she knew they were the ones who had looked after Sav while he had been trapped in his car.

She'd first seen Ted on that fateful day in Emergency. He'd come in and held her hand when everyone else had been too busy to and then later, months later, she'd listened to his evidence in the coroner's court. Listened as Ted and his partner Doug had retold, from their professional perspective, their version of the tragic events. And afterwards, when the coroner had delivered his findings, when the legal side of it had finally ended, when supposedly life should have started to move on, they'd come up and offered Isla their deepest condolences.

And now she had to look them in the eye.

'Thank you, Ted.' She gave a small, nervous smile. 'Doug, too. It's good to see you both again.'

'No worries, Isla.' Ted gave a small nod, glad she'd made the first uncomfortable move. Then he pulled her aside slightly, awkward formalities over and ready to concentrate on the patient. 'This is the little guy's third trip to hospital in a fortnight. Apparently his parents have just separated and the school's concerned that the stress at home might be causing the attacks.'

'Thanks for that.' Isla glanced over at the little boy, smiling cheerfully as his anxious teacher clucked around him. 'He doesn't look very stressed,' Isla said thoughtfully. 'How was he when you arrived at the school?'

'He had a slight wheeze, but apart from that he seemed OK.' Ted gave a shrug. 'It's hard to say, of course. The school had been giving him continuous Ventolin, so no doubt he'd improved a lot, but…' His voice trailed off and Isla gave a wry smile, neither wanting to be the one to cast the first stone. 'I'll get Reception to pull out his old admission notes for you while I register him,' Ted offered instead, and Isla gave a grateful nod. 'How are you doing?' Ted asked then, reverting to a rather more personal subject, his voice thickening in embarrassment, and Isla gave a rather noncommittal smile.

'Getting there,' she said, then gave a tiny, more honest sigh. 'Or, rather, I'm trying to get there.'

'You will,' Ted said gently. 'I know it's hard.'
Did he?

Did anyone who hadn't been through it really know just how hard it was? But, of course, Isla didn't say that. Instead, she forced a smile, said her goodbyes then headed back to her remarkably cheerful patient.

'How are you, Jamie?' Isla asked, checking his obs and listening to his chest as he chatted away with amazing fluency for someone who was supposed to be having an asthma attack.

'My chest still feels tight,' Jamie responded as Isla pulled off her stethoscope. 'Are my mum and dad here yet?'

'They're on their way,' Miss Symons soothed. 'I rang your mum myself.'

'And Dad,' Jamie checked. 'Did you ring my dad as well?'

'Your mum was going to do that,' Miss Symons answered, turning anxious eyes to Isla and nodding to the door, clearly wanting a quiet word out of Jamie's earshot. But Isla took a couple of moments to finish what she was doing and write down her observations before heading out of the cubicle.

'His asthma's got a lot worse since his parents broke up,' Miss Symons started as soon as Isla stepped outside. 'I know he looks fairly well now, but he was extremely breathless in the classroom. It was awful to watch, the other children were terrified.

'Now something really needs to be done.

Clearly his asthma isn't being properly controlled, the doctor who saw him last week only
kept him here for a couple of hours. I don't
think he understood me when I said that his
parents had separated and that Jamie was under
a lot of stress. He barely spoke English.'

'Do you remember the doctor's name?' Isla
asked.

'Something foreign—Salv, or something like
that. I really don't think he understood just
how bad Jamie had been in class. Surely he
needs to be admitted—'

'Problem?'

Isla bristled as Heath walked over. Even
though he'd apologized for his behaviour yesterday, even though he'd been nothing but nice
since, Isla quite simply couldn't take to him,
and it had nothing to do with what Sav or Jayne
had said. There was something behind those
cool glassy eyes and perfect smile that had the
hairs on the back of Isla's neck standing on
end.

'I was just explaining to the sister that the

doctor who saw Jamie the last two times seems rather dismissive. He doesn't seem to understand that—'

'Do we know who the doctor is?' Heath asked.

'I think it was Sav,' Isla responded, refusing to blush just because he was her husband. 'However, this isn't Jamie's mother, this is his teacher—'

'Who's naturally very concerned,' Heath broke in with a wide reassuring smile aimed at the teacher. Miss Symons melted on the spot. 'Let's take a look at the young man, shall we?'

Heath was very thorough in his examination, gently reassuring Jamie at every opportunity, talking in depth to his very anxious parents when they arrived and arranging a chest X-ray before asking the paediatricians to come and assess the young boy to arrange admission.

'Admission?' Isla deliberately removed the frown that had formed in her forehead as they walked back to the nurses' station. 'But he's well.'

'It's also his third presentation in less than a fortnight. Clearly something isn't right,' Heath pointed out. 'And, as the teacher said, he's improved markedly since the initial attack.'

'Who are we talking about?'

Nothing in Heath's stance changed, but Isla could have sworn she heard an annoyed intake of breath as Sav came over.

'My patient,' Heath responded tartly, clearly wishing to leave it there.

But Sav peered over his shoulder and, unlike Isla, did nothing to keep his frown hidden as he registered the name at the top of the chart.

'Jamie Chappell? Isn't that the little guy with the asthma who came in earlier in the week?'

'The one you discharged…' There was surliness behind Heath's voice that had Isla's senses on high alert. 'Despite the fact he'd presented a few days before with a similar episode.'

'Absolutely,' Sav responded firmly. 'There was no need for admission. He wasn't even wheezing when he got here. What's wrong with him today—another asthma attack?'

When Heath didn't answer, Isla stepped in. 'He became breathless at school, the teacher called for an ambulance, though according to the paramedics he wasn't particularly distressed when they got there.'

'Because he'd been on continuous Ventolin, as per the school's asthma protocol.' Heath bristled. 'Obviously he isn't being managed properly.' There was a challenge in Heath's voice. No matter how polite the conversation, Isla knew, just knew Heath was using a patient to prove a point. 'He should never have been discharged the last time.'

'In that case,' Sav responded, his the voice of reason as Isla found she was holding her breath, 'I'll see him again and make sure that I didn't miss anything last time.'

Taking the casualty card, Sav went to walk off but Heath called him back. 'Maybe that's not such a good idea, Sav. The teacher requested that another doctor see him…' Isla's mouth opened in protest. The teacher may not have been particularly complimentary about Sav but she certainly hadn't insisted on a different doctor. But from the warning look Sav shot in her direction, Isla took her cue and snapped her mouth closed. Clearly Sav didn't need her to fight his battles. 'I am the consultant.' For the first time since the unpleasant conversation had started, Sav's voice had an edge, a certain air of authority as he stared directly back at Heath. 'If the patient has been mismanaged then it is my responsibility, especially if I am the doctor who has twice discharged him.'

'Perhaps.'

Heath stared defiantly back and despite the warm hospital air suddenly Isla felt icy cold, the bristling hatred emanating from Heath clear now for all to see. She rued the times she had dismissed Sav's concerns, could have kicked herself for the times she had reassured him that Heath would come around, that it was all OK, when obviously it wasn't.

'The teacher also pointed out that you didn't seem to understand what was being said, that perhaps...' a hint of a smirk played on the edges of Heath's full mouth '…your English isn't quite up to the job.'

'And I'm sure you did nothing to reassure her.' Sav's eyes narrowed as he eyed his colleague. 'But what do you think, Heath? That's the real issue here after all. Do you think my English isn't up to the job? Do you think I'm so incompetent that I'd discharge an unstable asthmatic?'

'Of course not.' The sneer rapidly disappeared, the beginnings of a blush spreading in an unflattering swoop over Heath's cheeks as Sav faced the confrontation head-on.

'Because, if that is the case,' Sav continued, his voice icy calm, 'then we've got a real problem. We're supposed to be a team. For this place to survive we have to work as a team. We all have to respect each other, be there for each other. And as I'm the consultant and you're the senior registrar, if we can't depend on each other, it needs to be addressed.' He waited for Heath's response but none was forthcoming. 'Heath,' Sav snapped, 'is there a problem?'

'No.' Heath gave a tight shrug. 'Of course not.'

'Good,' Sav responded curtly. 'Did you read the previous admission notes on Jamie Chappell?' When Heath shook his head, Sav carried on. 'Well, in my conclusion I suggested that perhaps it wasn't Jamie's asthma that was the issue, but rather the school's and the family's response to it.'

'Do you think he's putting it on?' Isla asked, speaking for the first time, glad the conversation was moving back to Jamie.

'Not the first time,' Sav answered Isla, though his eyes never left Heath. 'When he first presented he was clearly having an asthma attack. We kept him here for six hours and he was started on a reducing dose of prednisolone. However, the next time he came in, apart from a slight cough on exertion, Jamie appeared to be enjoying the theatre of it all. Surely by now you know that for me to write something like that in my notes I'm more than confident of my findings.'

Heath gave a tiny, grudging nod.

'Now, if you don't mind, Heath, I'd like to have a look at Jamie before I *again* speak to his parents.'

'That's fine,' Heath responded, tight-lipped.

'Do you want me to come?' Isla offered, but Sav shook his head.

'I'll be fine.' He started to go, then changed his mind, and it was Isla's cheeks flaming as she suppressed a smile, knowing before he even said it what was about to come next. But, Isla conceded as Sav aimed below the belt, in this instance his rather sarcastic humour was undoubtedly merited. 'Actually, you'd better come, just in case Miss Symons uses any long words I may not understand.'

Sav's examination was just as thorough as Heath's had been, but his manner was much more laid-back, a sharp contrast to Jamie's anxious parents and teacher, who hovered nervously in the background.

'Isla.' Sav looked up and smiled. 'Could you, please, take Jamie's relatives to the interview room? I just want to have a quick chat with him and then I'll be along.'

'He might get upset if we leave,' Mrs Chappell said, and even though Sav's smile stayed in place his response was unequivocal. 'I shan't be long.'

The reluctant trio headed to the interview room and Isla hesitated as the rather overbearing Miss Symons pushed open the door, clearly assuming she should be present.

'Perhaps Mr Ramirez will want to talk to Jamie's parents alone,' Isla suggested as tactfully as she could. 'There's a coffee machine in the waiting room or you could go to the kiosk—'

'It's fine,' Mrs Chappell said quickly. 'I don't have a problem with Miss Symons being present.'

Mr Chappell's frown told Isla there *was* a problem, but after a moment's hesitation he gave a resigned nod and followed the two women into the interview room, sitting uncomfortably as they chatted away about Jamie's episode that morning.

Isla felt sorry for him.

Felt his exclusion.

It was a relief when Sav finally appeared.

'First of all…' he gave a brief smile but it had an official ring to it as he sat down and immediately commanded the situation '…I believe Miss Symons felt I was rather dismissive of Jamie's symptoms when I saw him last week.' His accent was very pronounced but his articulation was perfect as he stared directly at the teacher, who shuffled uncomfortably in her seat.

'You were just so relaxed, I just didn't feel you had grasped…'

Sav shook his head, turning his attention back to the parents. 'I take asthma very seriously. If I appeared relaxed, that was for Jamie's benefit. The very last thing an anxious child needs is an anxious doctor.'

'Or mother.' It was the first time Mr Chappell

had spoken, and even though he'd only said two words they had been laced with bitterness.

'So it's my fault, is it?' Mrs Chappell hissed.

'Well, it certainly isn't my fault! I haven't been allowed near him since we separated.'

'You were the one who had an affair,' Mrs Chappell retorted. 'You're the one who signed yourself off from this family when you went with that tart.'

Even Miss Symons, who'd been begging to be let in, seemed to want out now. The atmosphere in the room was so exquisitely uncomfortable Isla felt as if she were in a sauna, and it dawned on her that she'd almost forgotten this part of nursing…

Forgotten the unblinkered view into other people's lives nursing permitted, forgotten that it wasn't just the nursing aspect that made Emergency so interesting but the roller-coaster ride of emotion you embarked on every single day when you crossed the threshold of the ambulance bay.

'When did you last see your son, Mr

Chappell?' Only Sav appeared completely at ease, supremely in control as he guided the family through the minefield of emotion.

'I haven't been allowed to see him,' Mr Chappell answered nastily, but the venom in his voice was aimed at his wife. 'I haven't been allowed near him for six weeks now.'

'But you have seen him,' Sav pointed out.

'I haven't,' Mr Chappell retorted angrily. 'The only bloody time I get near him is when he's sick…' His voice trailed off and Isla looked up, blinking as the penny dropped, watching everyone's reactions as realization started to hit home.

'Jamie is a clever boy,' Sav said finally, when the silence had gone on long enough. 'He's worked out that the only way he can see his father is to have an asthma attack.'

'But he *was* sick,' Miss Symons refuted. 'He could hardly breathe!'

'You're a teacher, Miss Symons.' Sav gave a tactful smile. 'You were quite right to call an ambulance, and if it happens again, I don't expect you to hesitate because of what's been said in this room. It is not a teacher's job to diagnose her charges, and neither should it be. If a child is struggling to breathe, you *have* to call an ambulance. However...' his gaze was sterner now as he addressed the parents '...I would strongly suggest that, whatever problems you two are having, you come to some sort of arrangement where access visits are concerned. Unless Jamie's father is placing him in danger...'

'I'm not,' Mr Chappell broke in.

'Unless,' Sav said again, 'his father is placing him in danger, Jamie needs to see him. Jamie needs to know that just because his parents have separated, it doesn't mean he has lost his father.'

Mrs Chappell gave a small nod, clearly shocked at the turn of events. 'I never thought...' She gave a helpless shrug. 'I mean, I thought the asthma was because of what his father had done, that the stress of the separation—'

'Children are amazingly resilient,' Sav said

gently. 'A divorce isn't going to effect Jamie's health if it is handled properly. As long as he feels safe, as long as he knows that he has two parents who love him, two parents he can see, I'm sure he'll be OK.'

For the first time Mrs Chappell looked over at her husband, confusion, pain, guilt flickering in her eyes.

'I never intended…' she started, then shook her head when she couldn't go on.

'Neither did I.' Mr Chappell's voice was gruff, but it was loaded with emotion.

Maybe, Isla thought, maybe there was a chance that somehow they might even make it. 'Can I see him, Debbie?'

'Of course.' Silent tears rolled down her cheeks and even Miss Symons took her cue and stood up to leave, but Sav halted her.

'It's important you remember what I said. If Jamie or any student appears to be having an asthma attack, you have to call an ambulance.'

'I will, and thank you, Doctor.' She gave a small nod and then slipped out of the room.

'So what happens now?' Mrs Chappell's voice had lost the rather terse ring, accepting with shaking hands the handkerchief her husband handed to her. 'Should I take him home, tell him he can see his father…?'

'I think,' Sav said slowly, 'given the circumstances, that Jamie should be admitted. I want to be as certain as I can be that it isn't his asthma that is causing these attacks. If I'm right, I think that will help to give you the confidence to deal with this. And,' he added, 'I also think you two need some time alone to talk, away from Jamie.'

'I suppose you'll throw in a social worker for good measure.' Mr Chappell's dry joke brought a smile from Sav.

'Of course.' His smile dimmed, delivering as only Sav could a mixture of compassion and brutal honesty. 'You two really do need to get your act together, for Jamie's sake.'

'And we will.' On rather shaky legs Debbie Chappell stood up. 'I'd better go and see him.' She gave an embarrassed shrug and turned to wait for her husband. 'I mean, *we'd* better go and see him.'

'Do you think they'll make it?'

Sav's voice echoed her own thoughts when they were finally alone.

'Perhaps,' Isla said thoughtfully. 'It looks to me like there's still a lot of love there.' She also gave an embarrassed shrug, realizing with internal horror that she'd repeated her own solicitor's words. 'But, then, what would I know?' Glancing at her watch, she let out a small yelp. 'I was supposed to be off duty five minutes ago.'

'There's no rush.' Sav gave an easy smile. 'You've still got half an hour till the boys finish school.'

'It's just…' Isla started, but didn't elaborate. She'd been hoping to dash to the shops and grab something quick and easy for dinner before she picked the boys up. Preferably something that would look and taste fabulous as well, just to prove to Sav that she really could do it all. But there was nothing quick or easy about taking the twins shopping, especially when they were hot and thirsty after a day at school.

'Don't worry about dinner.' Again he seemed to read her mind. 'Why don't you give the kids something easy and I'll grab a curry for us on the way home?'

'Sav, you don't have to,' Isla started, but he didn't let her finish.

'I want to.' He stood up and suddenly the tiny shabby interview room seemed infinitely smaller, the delicious scent that filled the bathroom every morning, the bedroom every night, impinging on the workplace, giddy in its effect. The man she'd always loved was suddenly here again, pinning her with his eyes, melting her with his words, making every last thing suddenly OK again. 'You've been working, so the last thing you need is to go home and cook. Get the twins fed and to bed then have a nice long bath.' He gave that slow lazy smile that was for her eyes only. 'Maybe you could open a bottle of something nice and *I'll* see to dinner.'

She nodded dumbly, breathing him in as he stepped closer. And even though it was out of bounds, even if this was the workplace, the rules mattered not a scrap as he pulled her into his arms, his lips finding hers, moulding her burning flesh with a hunger that was mutual. She tasted him, revelling in him, because even if she'd kissed him before, even if they'd made love through this long lonely time, right here, right now it was different. This was nothing about comfort, nothing about familiarity and everything about passion, a passion that drenched every pore as her body dissolved into his. He dwarfed her with his height, his tongue cool and sharp as it explored the hollows of her throat, the rough scratch of his chin as he buried his face deeper, desire blazing in his eyes when finally he pulled away.

'We'll never be like that, will we?'

'Like what?'

'Like the Chappells.' There was an urgency

in his voice that tore at her soul. 'Too bloody blind to see what's in front of us, too proud and too messed up to fight for what we've got.

'And we've got so much, Isla.'

'Sav?' Her hand dusted his cheek, capturing the haughty face in her palm, forcing him to look at her, 'I love you,' she choked. 'I just can't stand to see you hurting so much, can't stand seeing you in so much pain and knowing that you won't let me help.'

'He's gone, Isla.' Tears swum in those proud, dignified eyes. 'Nothing can make that better. Nothing.'

And it wasn't much. In fact, it was barely nothing at all. But it was the closest he'd come to admitting his pain, the closest he'd ever let her in, and for Isla it was enough, that tiny glimpse enough to sustain her through whatever lay ahead.

'You were right to come back to work, Isla.' He stared down at her. 'And I'm sorry I was opposed to it. I just…' His voice trailed off but Isla pushed for more.

'Just what, Sav?'

'I was scared for you,' he said softly. 'I still am. I know how hard it can be sometimes, how easy it is to compare, how things you see here can bring it all back.'

Isla closed her eyes. If only he'd told her this before, if only he'd shared his reservations with her. Instead, she'd assumed it had been his male pride that had been holding her back from resuming her career, when all this time he'd been trying to protect her.

'I'm OK, Sav.' Her voice was shaky but her resolve was strong. 'I know coming back to work might be difficult at times, but it can't be as hard as staying at home.'

'I can see that now,' Sav said softly, letting her go regretfully as his pager shrilled in his pocket. He quickly turned it off.

'I'd better go.' Smiling up at him, Isla headed for the door, stunned, pleased, amazed at the change in him, the change in *them*. She'd gone back to work so she could end her marriage, yet it would appear it was the one thing that might just end up saving it.

'No cooking,' Sav reminded her, his hand closing around hers as she reached for the doorhandle. 'No talking either,' he said gruffly, closing his eyes as he held her one last time before she left to pick up the boys. He buried his head in her hair and inhaled deeply, dragging her deeper into him. 'At least, not about the big stuff. I need you tonight, Isla, I need it to be about us.'

And she understood, understood perhaps more than Sav did.

Doctor, nurse, daughter, son, parent, friend…

They were all of those.

But tonight they needed to be lovers.

CHAPTER SEVEN

'CAN we stay up till Dad gets home?' Luke asked, ever the optimist, despite Isla's frantic efforts to get the twins shepherded into bed.

'Daddy might be very late,' Isla answered, mentally crossing her fingers as she did so. 'You can see him in the morning. Now, come on—bed.'

'But it's Friday,' Harry pointed out, his truculent face appearing at the bathroom door, and not even a mass of toothpaste-induced bubbles could hide the pursed lips as he eyed his mother suspiciously. 'We always get to stay up late on Friday.'

'I know.' Taking a deep breath, Isla tried to keep her voice light. 'But you've had a busy week, what with Mummy going back to work and everything. And you know that you'll have a late night tomorrow at Nanny's…'

'But it's Friday,' Harry insisted, and Isla mentally threw the child-rearing books out of the window, deciding there and then that this particular seven-year-old needed a good dose of honesty.

'Yes, it's Friday, Harry, but Mum and Dad need some time alone together.' She watched as Harry's eyes widened. 'Mum and Dad want to have some grown-up time *alone*!'

'Sexy.' Luke giggled and Harry stared at her, clearly appalled.

'No,' Isla said evenly, swallowing her own giggle. 'It's way better than that, it's called romance. I'm going to have a frantic clean-up of your Lego that's all over the living-room floor and then, instead of cooking, I'm going to have a nice bath and hopefully your dad, when he's filling up with petrol, will buy me some pretty flowers and a decent DVD that doesn't have a single crime scene or a futuristic robot in sight, and while we're watching it we'll eat a curry that I haven't cooked.'

'What's romantic about that?' Harry huffed.

'Plenty.' Isla grinned. 'And I only hope when the two of you are six feet five and filling up your cars with petrol, you'll remember this conversation and stop to buy flowers for whoever it is that's waiting for you at home.'

Taking an inordinate amount of time to rinse his mouth, finally Harry looked up.

'If we promise to be quiet, can we read?'

'Where are they?' Sav asked, raising his eyebrows at the amazingly quiet and tidy house. Soft music was coming from the CD player, candles were flickering at the table as a slightly breathless Isla took the white take-away bags from him and clipped through to the kitchen in unfamiliar high heels.

'Pretending to be asleep,' Isla answered over her shoulder, impossibly shy all of a sudden. Which was ridiculous, she scolded herself as

Sav peeled off his jacket and loosened his tie. They'd been married for nine years, for heaven's sake, shared more curries than she could count, and even though their marriage wasn't exactly picture perfect, they still made love, so why on earth did she feel like a virgin on her first date?

'I'll open some wine,' Sav offered, but Isla gestured to the two glasses on the bench, her lipstick gracing one of the rims. Despite her head start, it had done nothing to steady her nerves, and her hands were shaking as she spooned the rice onto plates and attempted to scoop the chicken jalfrezi into the centre.

'Try and get some on the plate,' Sav teased, taking over with hands that were perfectly steady, oblivious to the utter frenzy his wife was in.

Or maybe not?

'You look nice.' He ran an approving eye over her pale grey dress, her newly washed hair, falling in a cloudy mass around her creamy shoulders, a face that had been way too pale for way too long now, younger, prettier somehow, with two spots of colour burning on her cheeks, those delicious eyes glittering as she tried and failed to look back at him.

And she almost shrugged, almost dismissed his compliment, but, feeling the weight of his stare, instead she dragged her eyes to his, her throat constricting as she witnessed at first-hand the utter adoration that blazed there. 'I wanted to look nice,' Isla admitted softly. 'For you.'

'Oh, God, Isla.'

His voice was a low rasp, a deep, almost guttural moan as he crossed the tiny space between them, pushed her against the kitchen bench, devoured her with hungry lips, his tongue forcing her lips apart, his hands running over the swell of her breasts, his arousal fierce and urgent pressing against the hollow of her stomach. It matched her own need, translated perfectly the confusing, scary but glorious emotions that were flooding back all of a sudden. That he wanted her had never been in question, but that he desired her, that she still moved him so, was all the impetus she needed to drive this moment further, to let him take her weight and lift her onto the bench. She twined her legs around him, kissing him back with a passion that had been missing for too long now, her neck arching back as he explored every hollow with his expert tongue, his hands sliding up her bare thighs, toying with the silk of her skimpy knickers, his fingers playing at the edges. And he could have taken her there and then and it wouldn't have been too soon, but sense prevailed for a tiny second. 'The boys,' Isla gasped. 'They might come in.'

'They wouldn't dare,' Sav growled, but feeling her tension he relented, but only for a second. He lifted her effortlessly, his manhood pressing firmly into her as he carried her through to the lounge, kicking the door shut with one impatient foot, then lowering her onto a chair and sliding it over to the door, the temporary barricade all Isla needed to let her own guard down again, to revel in the effect of his touch, the desire that had gripped them, unrelenting as he moved over her. But she needed to see him, her needy fingers wrestling with the buttons of his shirt until Sav pulled it over his head, tie and all. And it was as if she was seeing him for the first time. She took an indulgent moment to marvel at the toned muscular body she had permanent access to, the silky olive skin, the smattering of ebony hair teasing into a snaky line that pointed to his groin. Her fingers teased him as they moved ever downwards, wrestling with his zipper, the need to have him inside her utterly overwhelming both of them. Yes, there were times to take it slow at times to relish each other, to savour the moment, but right here and now they needed affirmation, confirmation…

'Isla.' His single word was ragged, bordering on apologetic as he tore her panties aside, plunged into her. But no excuse for fervour was needed when his need was hers, her stifled scream ecstatic as he delved inside, taking her to that one place only Sav could, riding high on the crest of his wave, her ankles coiling around each other, thighs trembling convulsively, until the weight of him descended on her, his head resting in her swollen breasts, his breathing ragged and short as the reality that always beckoned crept back in.

'I miss you, Isla.'

They were the loneliest words she'd ever heard.

'I miss us.'

'I know.' Her whisper reached him, his face moving that tiny but infinite space to hers.

And she wanted to tell him, wanted to admit how close he'd come to losing her, to ending the nine-year dream that had turned into a nightmare.

But she couldn't.

Couldn't threaten this fragile flame of hope with the cold bluster of reality.

'Mummy.' An impatient voice broke the moment in the sweetest of ways.

'So it's Mummy now,' Isla grumbled, frantically pulling her dress down as Sav hastily grappled with his trousers. 'Coming, Harry!' she called in the brightest, happiest voice she could summon as Sav swiftly moved the chair.

'The door was jammed!' Harry protested, stomping in and staring at them both accusingly.

'I know. Daddy's going to fix it tomorrow,' Isla flustered, as a rather red-faced Sav headed to the kitchen. 'Why are you up at this time?'

'My tooth came out.'

'Wow!' Isla over-enthused as Harry showed her his new gap. 'You'd better put it under your pillow, then.'

'Why?'

'For the tooth fairy,' Isla answered, trying desperately to keep her voice normal.

'Tooth fairy!' Harry rolled his eyes, then quickly thought better of it, a shrewd smile lighting his face. 'Kevin Miller got three dollars from the tooth fairy last week.'

'Tell you what, Harry,' Sav returned, their two forgotten glasses in hand. He handed one to Isla, a rather rumpled T-shirt very out of place with charcoal grey pinstriped trousers. 'If you get back to bed and stay there, I'll up it to four dollars!'

'Five,' Harry pushed, clearly sensing weakness.

'Five, then,' Sav relented. 'So long as you don't wake Luke on the way back to bed.'

'A businessman in the making.' Isla grinned as Harry gave her a quick kiss and scampered back to bed. 'You don't think he heard anything?'

'Serve him right if he did.' Sav shrugged, but his normally deadpan face darkened with a blush as it screwed into an embarrassed wince. 'He wouldn't have, would he?'

Never had tepid curry tasted so good.

A light romantic film in the background, the glass of heavy red replaced with iced water and Sav adoring her with his eyes.

'I'm sorry.'

His apology wasn't that unexpected and Isla's

breath caught in her throat as she looked back at him.

'I know I've been hell to live with, I know I've shut you out, I just…' His voice trailed off but Isla pushed on, determined to build on this new closeness, determined to forge a new start for both of them.

Determined to make this work.

'Just what, Sav?' Her voice was gentle, her eyes sympathetic, and after the longest pause he gave a small nod.

'You remember how my mother cried when I said I wanted to live in Australia?' He took a long sip of his water before continuing, and Isla nodded as she remembered. Those innocent, happy times when the world had lain at their feet, on the brink of a thousand tomorrows with the certainty their love would see them through whatever lay ahead. 'I told her that it was the right thing to do, that I loved you, wanted to make you happy, and that in turn it would bring her joy. I told your father the same thing when

I asked if I could marry you…' Tortured eyes met hers. 'No one's happy, Isla.'

'That isn't your fault,' she said urgently, and Sav gave a tired nod.

'I know that. Sometimes I don't really believe it, but deep down I know it is true. If the accident had been my fault, I couldn't…' His voice faltered, his eyes closing for a painful second. 'But whatever way you look at it, I've failed in keeping my promise. I hear the grief in my mother's voice, see the pain in your father's face. He's aged, Isla. In this last year he's aged a decade.'

'I know.' Tears brimmed in her eyes as she recalled her father's dull eyes, the sparkle in them seemingly gone for ever.

'I'm a doctor,' Sav said simply. 'I'm supposed to be able to fix things to make people feel better, yet all around me, in the people I care about the most, I see pain. My job was to make you happy, and when the boys came along, my job was to make them feel loved and safe.'

'Sav.' Tears swam in her eyes, but she held

them back, pleased despite the pain that this difficult, proud man was finally opening up. 'When Casey died I thought I'd never smile again let alone be happy. I couldn't imagine a single second when I wouldn't be engulfed, couldn't envisage a future without my baby. *Couldn't*,' she said again, more forcibly. 'And then one day I found myself smiling at something Luke said, and after a while I found I'd gone a few minutes without wanting to scream.' She watched his reaction, tried to read the expression in his veiled eyes. 'The pain was still there but somehow joy had started to trickle in. I'm starting to understand that the pain's always going to be there—always,' she said. Sav gave a slow, loaded nod. 'But slowly the good times have started to last a little bit longer, come a little more frequently, and one day I hope they'll outweigh the bad.'

'I hope so, too.'

Isla could almost feel him slipping away then, the barriers going up again. Only this time Isla didn't mind, understood perhaps that this wasn't something that could be resolved in a single conversation, that, like Sav, she didn't have the power to fix it.

But she could be there.

And later, lying beside him, nestled in the crook of his arm, being held close the way only Sav ever could, Isla knew she'd never have left him.

Knew in that moment that the trips to Karin Jensen, the frantic search for a supposed cure, had been her own knee-jerk response, had stemmed from her own desperate desire to make it all better, to rewind the world to when it had all been OK.

CHAPTER EIGHT

'WHERE'S Sav, darling?' Flattening herself against the front door as the boys flew past, Carmel Howard smiled as Isla finished speaking to the taxi driver then came up the garden path.

'He went to get a hair cut around two o'clock,' Isla answered, rolling her eyes. 'Then he rang to say he was stuck at the hospital and that if he didn't get back I was to make my own way there and he'd meet me.'

'Well, don't pay for a taxi. Your father can take you.'

'Where is Dad?' Isla asked, peering over her mother's shoulder into the lounge room, trying to ignore the sinking feeling in her stomach as

Carmel pinked up a little bit and avoided her daughter's eyes.

'He's just having a little lie-down. I'll go and get him.'

'Let him rest, Mum.' Deliberately, Isla kept her voice light. 'It's really no problem. Anyway, you'll probably need both of you to deal with the twins later, they're thoroughly over-excited of course.'

'And hungry, I hope,' Carmel said. 'We're going to take them to the new pizza place that's opened, it's got a massive—'

'Playground.' Isla grinned. 'I know. The boys begged me to take them there. They'll have a ball.'

'Hopefully it will cheer up your father,' Carmel said, and Isla didn't answer.

Couldn't answer.

Glimpsing Sav's pain again, the guilt, the agony that was eternally rammed home.

'Go,' Carmel urged, forcing a smile. 'You look fabulous.'

'I actually feel it.' Isla smiled. 'Well, not fabulous exactly, but pretty damned good.'

'Enjoy tonight. Heaven knows, you two deserve it.'

'We will, if Sav ever gets there. Boys, come and give me a kiss.'

They gave her three each, and an extra cuddle for luck, three smiling faces waving her off as Isla climbed into the taxi. The curtains fluttered upstairs, catching her eye, and she waved up at her father. Peter Howard duly smiled and waved back, but even from this distance Isla knew the smile didn't meet his eyes, could feel the lethargy in his movements, and she wished again fruitlessly that there was something she could do, something she could say, to make everything better.

The Docklands was a new development and Isla, along with the taxi driver, had never been before, but finally after a few moments poring over the *Melways*, which was a street directory of the city and a bible to every Melburnian motorist, they found what they were looking for.

'You'll have to walk the rest, love!' the taxi driver commented, peering out at the bustling walkways, utterly devoid of a basic necessity like a road! 'Do you know where you're going?'

'Not really,' Isla replied, more cheerfully than she felt. 'I'll be fine, though.'

Taking her time, she walked along, admiring the high-rise luxury apartments and smart shops, the abundance of trendy bars filled with even trendier people. She wished Sav was beside her as she hated walking into packed restaurants alone, though it was par for the course when married to a busy doctor, but even after nine years she'd never really got used to it.

'Over here, Isla.' Jayne's loud shout greeted her as soon as she walked in. Gratefully Isla bypassed the rather snooty doorman and the impatient queue of hungry people waiting to be seated, and made her way over to the loudest table in the place! It looked more like a combined hen and bucks night than a work do, but that was pretty much the unspoken rule when Emergency staff got together and partied. The stress of such a demanding job ensured that downtime was taken very seriously and the evening ahead would undoubtedly achieve in a few short hours what the work counsellors attempted.

Good food, good wine and a good dose of black humour were very much the order of the day here!

'Where's Sav?' Jayne asked, filling a glass of wine without prompting and handing it to Isla.

'He should be here soon.' Isla shrugged, rolling her eyes and taking a sip of her drink, then pulling a face. 'So long as nothing big comes in.'

'Where would the hospital be without Sav?'

Heath's smile didn't quite drown out the sarcasm, and Isla felt her stomach tighten with nerves as Heath raised a glass. His eyes had a dangerous glint to them and, Isla guessed, he'd either been drinking before he'd got here or was making up for lost time, signalling rather impatiently for the waiter to fill up his glass as he stared openly at Isla. Suddenly an evening of drinking didn't hold much appeal. Heavy wafts of garlic were drifting from the kitchen and, mingling with her nerves, it wasn't the most steadying cocktail so Isla decided to give the wine a miss, instead signalling a waiter and asking for a jug of water and a large glass of cola.

'So, how are you finding everyone?'

'Marvellous,' Isla gulped, and then forced a smile, wishing someone else would turn and talk to her, wishing she could be anywhere other than sitting opposite this menacing man. 'Everyone's been great.'

'Of course, you'd know them already.' Still he stared. 'It would just be a matter of putting names to faces.'

'Sorry?' Isla frowned.

'I'm sure Sav's spoken about us all—Jayne, the efficient, friendly but slightly insipid charge nurse, Jordon, the dependable but slightly anxious registrar, and, of course, Heath.' He let out a low laugh. 'I can just imagine what he said about me. Well?'

'Well what?' Isla responded, annoyed now and refusing to be dragged into his games.

'Have I lived up to my reputation? Am I as arrogant and incompetent as Sav suggested?'

'Heath!' Picking up on the tension, Jayne turned, her eyes swivelling between the two of them then landing squarely on Heath. 'It's supposed to be a friendly night out…'

'It's OK, Jayne.' Isla put her hand up. She didn't need Jayne diving in and saving her. She'd been through too much in her life for this obnoxious, difficult man to even register a blip on her pain scale. 'Contrary to what you clearly believe, Heath, you're really not at the top of our list of topics to discuss. We happen to have a life outside the emergency room.' She watched as he swallowed the drink he was holding in his mouth and almost left it there, almost turned her back and spoke to Jayne.

And for the rest of her life she would wish that she had.

'I form my own opinions, Heath,' Isla said slowly, taking a measured sip of her own drink but still holding him with her eyes. 'Arrogant? Yes,' she said softly but firmly. 'Incompetent?' Placing her drink on the table, she gave a tiny shrug. 'The jury's still out.'

'Here's Sav.' The appalling mood lifted suddenly as half the table announced his arrival, and Isla's eyes jerked gratefully to the door, her heart stilling for a long moment as she watched him enter.

He stood a good head above everyone else. His dark hair had been cut, but slightly differently this time, still the usual smart, short back and sides but the fringe had been left longer, flopping over his forehead. He'd been home and changed, the casual shorts replaced with black jeans. The white T-shirt, which had to be new—unless her laundering skills had upped a considerable notch—was half-tucked into his jeans, showing a thick black belt, and as he walked over she had to sit on her hands not to reach out to him, had to literally hold herself back from running to him.

He was quite simply the most beautiful man she had ever seen.

And from the slightly pink glow to more than a few of her colleague's cheeks, Isla wasn't the only one who thought so.

Sav Ramirez was one of those men who could bring a room to a standstill. He had a commanding presence, effortlessly sexy yet still approachable, and the years had done nothing to diminish his beauty. If anything, they had accelerated it. There was the wisdom behind those dark eyes, a distinguished aura that set him apart, and the best bit of all, Isla realized as he unashamedly came over to her, completely at ease he kissed her full on the mouth, his hand snaking around her waist before turning to face the crowd, the best bit of all—he was hers.

'We've ordered!' Lydia, one of the younger, louder nurses laughed as Sav slipped into the bench beside Isla. 'Lots of everything, so we can all pile in and share.'

'Sounds good.' Sav nodded, smiling up at the suddenly attentive waiter, who seemed to realize that the head of the table had just arrived.

'Can we have some champagne?' Sav asked, without checking with everyone else, 'and maybe some dips to mop it up before the meals start to arrive.'

This was certainly the place for dips! Thick, warm strips of Turkish bread appeared as if by magic and the whole table promptly fell on them, dipping them in the richest dips that over and over mocked the bland attempts from the supermarket. They were thick with garlic and lemon juice, a thousand taste sensations with each and every mouthful, and Isla let out a low groan of approval as she reverted back to the hummus.

'Save space for the main course,' Sav said, but Isla shook her head.

'It couldn't be better than this.'

Wrong!

As the table got louder the food got better, smoky chicken meatballs, firmly entrenched on Isla's new list of favorites as Sav found out that Lebanese pizza was *almost* as good as Spanish.

'High praise indeed.' Isla laughed. 'And these meatballs are definitely better than your mother's.'

'Nothing could be better than my mother's,' Sav corrected tartly, then grinned to show he was joking. 'It's not just the food, though, is it?'

'No,' Isla admitted. It wasn't.

It was about being here with him.

About getting not out of the house but out of their grief, even if only for a small time. About slowly dipping their toes into a world that had been out of bounds for so long now and finding that the water wasn't as cold as it looked, that it was actually quite warm and inviting.

'It's not even about the company,' Isla added, when their rather dewy-eyed stare had gone on too long, considering they were out in com-

pany. Her rather pointed eye roll in the direction of Heath had Sav
frowning for a second.

'What was going on when I got here?'

'Nothing,' Isla said, too lightly. Realizing she couldn't fool Sav, she gave a small shrug. 'We had words.'

'What sort of words?'

'I don't know,' Isla admitted. 'It wasn't so much what was said, more the way it wasn't said, if that makes any sense.'

'Not much,' Sav replied, 'but given you've had the best part of a bottle of champagne I'll forgive you.'

'I've had half a glass,' Isla corrected, shaking her head as Sav went to top her up. 'I'm not really in the mood to drink.'

'Watch him, Isla.' Sav's voice had a low note of urgency as he replaced the bottle on the table. 'He doesn't like you.'

'Why?' Isla blinked. 'What have I ever done to him?'

'Nothing. It's dislike by association, I'm

afraid. I have the two things Heath wanted most.'

'Two things?' Isla frowned. 'I know he wanted the consultant's position, but what's the other thing?'

'A happy marriage.' He watched as her frown stayed, his hand moving over hers and tightening. She could feel the warmth of his skin on hers and, most terrifying of all, given where they were, feel the sharp sting of tears behind her eyes. 'It's still that, isn't it, Isla?'

'Not here, Sav.' She shook her head slightly.

'OK.' His voice was steady and low, but she could hear the emotion behind it as he carried on talking. 'But it will be again, Isla, I promise you that. Maybe happy wasn't the greatest choice of words, but it is strong.' He paused for a second before carrying on, his eyes lifting to the bar where Heath was noisily demanding a drink. 'Watch him, Isla. I don't like him, I don't trust him and I don't respect him, and the most dangerous part of it all is that he knows that.'

'What are you going to do?' Worried eyes

met his. 'I mean, you work together, you have to be able to—'

'Not here.' It was Sav rightly halting the conversation now, a work do hardly the place for an in-depth discussion. 'Just be careful, that's all.'

'Heath!' Jayne's angry voice had them both looking over as Heath returned, knocking over a couple of glasses as he did so.

'Sorry.' Heath slumped in the seat opposite as Jayne attempted to mop up the mess. 'Sorry,' he said again. 'It's just I've been racking my brains since Thursday.' His attention swivelled to Isla, who sat uncomfortably trying to ignore him. 'Over and over I've been trying to place where I knew you from and finally I've got it.'

'Got what?' Sav's voice was icy, his disapproval evident as he eyed his drunken colleague.

'Where I know her from,' Heath slurred. 'Well, not know her exactly, but where I've seen her. The solicitor's office—Jensen and Webster's, the "happy family" law specialists.'

Isla felt her stomach turn to liquid, the room that had been pleasantly warm stifling now as beads of sweat formed on her forehead, icy rivers of sweat trickling between her breasts, watching as Sav's hand tightened around his fork, his eyes narrowing for a second as Heath relentlessly continued.

'On Wednesday, you were behind me at the recep-tionist's desk. It was you, wasn't it? Tell me, Isla, what would a happily married woman like you be doing at a solicitor's that special-izes in family law?'

She didn't answer, just sat there as the table fell silent. She stared at the mountain of food on her plate and suddenly felt sick.

'They also deal with wills.' Sav's voice was so nonchalant, so laid-back that for an impos-sible second Isla almost believed what she was hearing. 'We've recently updated our wills, Heath—not, of course, that it's any of your business.'

'Of course not,' Heath flustered, 'I was just saying...'

'Given our circumstances,' Sav snapped, his voice not quite so nonchalant now, 'it's hardly the most cheerful of subjects for a night out, so perhaps we'll leave it there, huh?'

'Of course,' Heath mumbled, his ruddy alcohol-induced flush darkening as the entire table eyed him coolly, a few sympathetic glances being cast in Isla's direction. She neither wanted nor deserved them, but they didn't know that.

Only two people present knew she hadn't been there to amend her will.

Sav and herself.

She could only admire him as he waded through the meal and then finally, thankfully sipped on his dark sweet coffee, then signed the bill with a flourish, cracking a joke or two as he carefully deducted the champagne and dips and added them to his portion before dividing up the rest.

And Isla played her part, too.

She kissed a few cheeks, laughed at some corny jokes, even held Sav's hand as they said farewell to the rowdy table and stepped out into the cool night air outside. She stared for a trembling moment at the shimmering waterways that surrounded them, shivering as Sav jangled his keys in his pocket and, undoubtedly for the effect of the gathered crowd in the window behind them, placed a casual arm around her shoulders as he guided her to the car park. But she could feel the tension in his touch. His fingers barely touched her but seemed to bite into her flesh as on they walked, his breath hard and ragged as they walked the agonizing distance.

'Sav!' she started when finally they were round the corner, stopping in her tracks and pulling on his arm. 'Sav, please, if you'll just let me—'

'Shut up.' It was hardly big league and given the circumstances utterly and completely merited, but such was the snarl with which the two words were delivered, Isla stepped back as if she'd been hit, choking back a sob as Sav picked up her hand and practically marched her to the car. Her heels echoed around the multi-storey car park and she vaguely registered a couple embracing beside the lift, the world rolling ever on as hers fell apart.

'Get in.' There was nothing gentlemanly about the way he held the door open and Isla sat holding her breath as Sav walked around to the driver's side, slamming the door and pulling on his seat belt.

'We have two children.' His fingers gripped the steering-wheel, tension in every muscle as he dragged in a long steadying breath, his eyes staring fixedly ahead as he spoke. 'I owe it to them to drive safely.'

Teeth chattering, she nodded, screwing her eyes closed as Sav continued.

'But when we get home, Isla, we'll have that talk you've been after for so long.'

For the first time since Heath had dropped his bombshell his black eyes actually managed to meet hers.

'Believe me, Isla, we'll talk.'

* * *

'Well?' His voice was as loud as the front door that slammed behind them, and Isla felt relieved that the twins were at her parents', that they could say what needed to be said without fear of waking them.

And so much needed to be said.

'I did go to see a solicitor,' she started nervously, following Sav through to the living room, wishing he would just sit down, that they could both sit down and talk this through, but knowing it was a wasted wish. Sav, tall and proud and defensive, paced the room like a trapped animal, his face jerking towards her every now and then, his eyes demanding answers.

'I know that, Isla, the whole of bloody Emergency knows that. The question is, what were you doing there?'

A dry tongue ran over even drier lips. She mentally berated Heath over and over for his part in this, for forcing out a truth that she'd sworn to keep inside, yet knowing deep down that she only had herself to blame.

'I went to see about a divorce.'

'A divorce?' Sav's voice was amazingly calm. His pacing halted for a moment, his expression bordering on reasonable as he faced her. 'Why do you want a divorce?'

'I don't.' Her throat felt as if it were full of sand, every sense on high alert as her mind struggled with how to play this, knowing that every word she uttered mattered.

'Then what the hell were you doing at a solicitor's?'

'I thought that was what I wanted, Sav. When I first went to see Karin I couldn't see any way out…'

'First?' He pounced on the word as Isla mentally kicked herself. 'It wasn't the first time?'

'No.' Her legs were trembling violently now and out of necessity she sat down, her eyes pleading with him to follow her, but still he stood, watching as she ran a shaky hand through her hair then over her eyes.

'When I went the first time, I was desperate. I'd tried to talk to you, tried to tell you how I was feeling, and we'd had a massive row. The twins had been crying because you wouldn't talk about Casey—'

'Leave them out of this,' Sav snapped. 'This is about you and me, Isla. Don't try to hang this on them.'

'I'm not,' Isla said, her voice more forceful now. 'But, like it or not, Sav, this *does* affect them. I couldn't deal with it, I couldn't see any other way, but when I went back, when it actually came down to it, I knew I couldn't go through with it, knew that it wasn't what I wanted.'

The longest silence followed, broken only by his breathing, her own pulse hammering in her temples as she awaited the next inevitable onslaught.

'Why did you go back to work?' He stared at her coolly as Isla struggled to answer.

'So I could support myself.'

'Did you think that I wouldn't?'

'I knew you would.' Tear-filled eyes looked up at him. 'But I didn't want to be a burden.'

'Save the tears, Isla,' he said nastily. 'So all the little speeches you gave about being bored during the day, about needing more to fill your time, were just rubbish?'

'No.' She gave a helpless shrug. 'Maybe at first, but as soon as I was back at work I knew it was the right thing to do, that it was what I needed after all. What we both needed, Sav. Since I've been back at work things have been better between us.'

'You've only been back two days,' Sav pointed out, but Isla shook her head.

'It *has* been better,' she insisted.

'I don't get it.'

His coolness was unnerving her. She'd expected an explosion, for that Latin temper to blister through the house, like hot molten lava destroying everything in its wake, to be ripped apart by his savage tongue. But instead, though clearly angry, Sav was amazingly calm and controlled, firing questions relentlessly, cross-examining her over and over, never missing a beat, as she sat there shivering in her own misery.

'Why, when you're planning to divorce me, would you even think about taking a job in my department? For crying out loud, as if three shifts are going to support you and the children. What sort of solicitor would tell you to go back to work?'

'She told me not to,' Isla responded, choking back tears, wishing fervently that she'd had a drink after all so that she could face this onslaught with some numbness. But there was no anaesthetic that could save her from the cold hard truth and Isla had to face it. 'She told me that the very last thing I should do was go back to work.'

'So why did you?' Sav pushed, completely unmoved by her obvious emotion. 'Are you going to try and sit there and tell me that you were worried about me, that it was so you could keep an eye on me?'

'No.'

'So that we could stay close for the sake of the children?'

'No.'

'Because, Isla, you can forget amicable, you can forget nice…' Suddenly she was reminded of Karin's words, could feel herself being dragged back into the circle of hatred she'd witnessed in the office, the one she'd forcibly pulled herself back from. 'If you take my kids away from me, if you rip apart my family by walking away, the last thing I'll be is nice. The last thing I'll be is one of those people who puts on a nice front for the sake of the kids, one of those—'

'Sav, please…' Isla begged, hating this glimpse of a future she didn't want.

'Why, Isla?' he barked. 'Why the hell did you take this job?'

'Because it was the only one that would give me the shifts I wanted. I thought that once I had some more experience, I'd go to the new hospital once it opened. This was supposed to be a stopgap…'

'So you were using them? They're desperate for staff, they've bent over backwards to accommodate you, and all the time you were intending to walk away.'

'It wasn't like that,' Isla said, but Sav wasn't listening.

'So you were lying to them the same way you've been lying to me all this time! My God, Isla, I don't even know you. I'm standing here looking at you and I don't even recognize you!'

She waited, waited for the next round, bracing herself for the firing of more questions, but nothing, nothing prepared her for what came next. Nothing prepared her for the pounding of his feet on the stairs, the horrible sight, as she burst into the bedroom, of him angrily filling a case.

'Sav, don't,' she begged. 'We need—'

'To talk?' This time he did shout, this time anger laced every word. 'Talk to me through your solicitor.'

'Sav, I don't want a divorce. I don't want it be over.' Her hands pulled at the garments, pulling out socks and T-shirts as he threw them in. But he brushed her hands away, slammed the lid of the case closed without even looking at her. 'When I saw Karin I was confused. I just wanted, wished—'

'You should be more careful what you wish for, Isla.' Lifting the case, he walked smartly to the door.

'Sav, please, don't go. Not like this…'

'What do you care?' Appalled, he stared at her, shaking his head as if he didn't know her.

'I care because I love you.'

'Not good enough.' Again he shook his head and it was Isla's turn to be angry. Yes, she'd been wrong, but not entirely without reason. Her mind spun back to the silence he had induced, the long lonely tension-filled nights, the wobble in Luke's normally sunny voice when he spoke about his father.

'You did this, too, Sav.' She stared defiantly back at him. 'You shut me out for so long I didn't know where to turn. We can't even say Casey's name in this house any more.'

'You're being ridiculous.'

'I'm telling the truth. Since the day he died you haven't ever spoken his name, and now the kids don't either—at least, not when you're around.'

'Bull.'

'Say it, then.' She stared at him, defiant eyes filling now, her face crumpling as he stood proud and angry and utterly immovable.

'There's nothing to say.' His lips barely moved. One final glare and he turned on his heel. 'I'm going to a hotel.'

'No.' She lunged after him, frantic, appalled, scarcely able to believe this was really happening, trying to stall him, saying the first thing that came to her mind. 'What if the hospital rings?'

'Tell them.' He glowered. 'They're going to find out soon enough!'

'And the kids?' Isla begged. 'What do I tell them?'

'Whatever you've been planning,' Sav shouted, but it changed midway into an almost strangled plea. 'We made love yesterday, Isla, we made love, and all the while you were planning—'

'I wasn't!'

'How the hell am I supposed to ever trust you? We made love!' he reiterated, anger, hurt and confusion in every word.

Isla truly didn't know how to respond, but it didn't matter because Sav had plenty to say. Sav shouting out the final words as he stormed down the stairs and wrenched open the front door. 'You started this.

'And I'm finishing it!'

If the row had been hell, hearing the door slam, the angry skid of Sav driving off, her sobs filling the empty house inflicted a pain that was indescribable. Backed into a corner, he'd come out fighting, that fierce Mediterranean pride taking over as Isla had known it would.

And like a shock victim, Isla wandered from room to room, staring blindly at the photos that littered every surface, the faces smiling back at her—not just the children's, but Sav's and hers, younger, thinner, more vibrant, mocking her over and over with their innocence. There was no refuge in the bedroom either, the marital bed out of bounds now. She paced the floor, phone in hand, fighting the urge to ring him, to beg him to see reason, yet knowing it would be futile, that nothing she could say tonight would penetrate. She couldn't face the twins' room, couldn't picture their lonely faces when she told them the appalling news. Finally she fixed on the one room that should have hurt her but curiously didn't, the one room where she could almost find peace, the peace she craved. She flicked on the nightlight and curled up on the bed like a wounded animal, staring at the teddies that smiled down at her, watching the clowns that danced on the ceiling, chasing away the nightmares and promising that things would all seem better in the morning.

CHAPTER NINE

THANK God for friends.

Thank God for the women who could banish a pile of school uniforms waiting to be ironed and children needing to bathed, nails needing to be cut and a husband waiting to be fed, and come over at a moment's notice when they were really needed.

Mug after endless mug of coffee appeared as if by magic, as eighteen hours later the problem seemed no clearer.

'Have you told your parents?' Practical as ever, Louise fussed around the kitchen, piling sandwiches and fruit into the boys' lunchboxes for the morning, then dragging out the ironing board and setting to work.

'I couldn't.' Isla gave a helpless shrug. 'Dad

just looked so old and tired and jaded, I just couldn't bring myself to say anything.'

'And the twins?' Louise lowered her voice needlessly. The boys were tucked up in bed, happily oblivious to the appalling events that had taken place.

'No.' Taking a sip of coffee, Isla was jerked out of her introspection for a second. 'What's in this?'

'Chocolate,' Louise said crisply. 'You need it.'

Did she ever!

'We need to do that together. Once Sav calms down, he'll do what's right. I'm not going to tell them just yet.'

'Good.' Louise paused for the longest time, scorching a V into a white shirt as she stared at her friend. 'I understand about the kids, I even understand why you couldn't tell your parents today, but what I don't understand is why the hell you couldn't tell me, Isla. We're supposed to be friends.'

'We are,' Isla insisted, but Louise gave a confused shake of her head.

'We tell each other everything, well, maybe not everything, but I was the one who made your hair appointment that day. How could you *forget* to mention you were seeing a solicitor?'

It was a good question and one Isla wrestled with before answering, red-rimmed, swollen eyes finally looking up from her coffee cup. 'I guess if I told you, it was real.' Isla swallowed, but the lump in her throat remained. 'And I didn't want it to be.'

'Oh, Isla!' Somehow Louise had the foresight to pull the plug out of the iron before heading across the kitchen and embracing her friend. 'You know I love you, you know how much I care, and I know Sav's been difficult and impossible and hell to live with, but—and don't hate me for saying this—you have been, too.'

'I thought you were my friend.' Isla's words weren't quite as pathetic as they sounded, delivered with a wobbly smile as she delved in her mug for the chocolate at the bottom.

'I *am* your friend,' Louise said firmly. 'And since Casey died I've read up a bit on grief. Look, I know I'm not a nurse or a doctor but I do know that grief comes in stages. What stage is Sav at?'

'Guilt,' Isla sighed. 'Denial, anger—take your pick.'

'And what about you?'

Isla frowned into her coffee, not liking the way the conversation was turning.

'Acceptance,' she said finally. 'I've run the full gauntlet and now I'm at acceptance.'

'No, Isla.' Louise shook her head, her eyes kind but firm, the arms of friendship still wrapped around Isla as they told the truth the way only a real friend could. 'You're at the bargaining stage.'

'No…' Isla started, shaking her head in refusal, but Louise continued. 'Bargaining. If Sav will just open up, things will be better. If I go back to work, things will get back to normal. If I go and see a solicitor and hit Sav with the threat of divorce, I'll snap him out of his misery.'

'That's about Sav and me,' Isla refuted. 'It has nothing to do with Casey.'

'Yes, it does,' Louise said slowly, gripping Isla's hands as they shredded a mound of tissues. 'What then, Isla? Snap Sav out of his misery and everything will be what?'

Isla shook her head, dragged the chair an inch and went to stand, but Louise held her down.

'Be what, Isla?'

'Normal again,' Isla whispered, her teeth chattering around the words. 'I just want it all to be normal again.'

'It will be,' Louise promised, tears streaming down her own face now. She didn't even bother to wipe them away. 'But a different type of normal. You can run around chasing what you had for ever, but it isn't going to happen. Things are never going to be the same for your little family again.'

And it was horrible and painful and awful, but true. Isla wept choking tears, mourning, as if for the first time, not just a little boy who had died but the loving family that had gone with him.

'So, what now?' Isla asked, when her nose was raw, her eyes so red and swollen she could see her own lids. 'What do I do now? Sav's never going to—'

'Sav loves you, just as much as you love him,' Louise said wisely. 'Talk to him—'

'I've been trying.'

'Then listen,' Louise said gently.

'He doesn't say anything.'

'Then keep on listening, and even if all you get is silence for a while, keep right on. Sooner or later he'll open up.'

Which sounded like a plan.

Not much of a plan but enough to get her caffeine-overloaded body into bed and her confused mind to drift into a brief a semblance of sleep, to force unconsciousness until a bleary face greeted her.

'You've overslept!'

'I haven't,' Isla mumbled, groping for her

alarm clock, taking solace in the fact that the bedroom was way too dark for her to be late. But as her eyes finally focused and her ears registered the rumbling thunder and pounding rain against the window, Isla realized that Harry was spot on.

They were going to be late!

Still, the mad rush to get two boys washed, dressed and fed and find raincoats that hadn't been seen in six months was gratefully received, as were the uniforms laid out on the couch and the lunchboxes Louise had neatly stacked in the fridge. Gratefully received because in her haste to get them all ready, Isla had no time to think the unthinkable. She even managed to sound vaguely normal as she ordered Luke back to the bathroom to *really* brush his teeth this time and tucked in Harry's permanently untucked shirt.

'Where's Dad?' He was so intent on trying to tie up his own shoelaces, Harry didn't see Isla's nervous swallow.

'He got called in to work, so Louise will be

taking you both to school this morning.' And she waited, waited for some suspicious comment, but thankfully it never came.

'Can I have sixty cents for the tuck shop?'

'I haven't got any change.'

'A dollar, then?'

Maybe not such a businessman, Isla thought, scrabbling down the sides of the sofas and duly pulling out a dollar for each of them. Right then Isla would have parted with the fifty-dollar note in her purse just to get out of the door.

Handover had already started as Isla slid to a rather apologetic halt, her hair drenched and dripping from her dash across the car park. She mouthed an apology to Jayne as the night sister frowned at her late arrival—and with good reason. The place was fit to burst and the last thing they needed, Isla realized as she frantically tried to catch up with the handover, was an emergency nurse with her mind elsewhere. It was her first Monday morning in Emergency for the best part of a decade, but nothing had changed. Sports injuries and hangovers. The penalties of a good weekend groaned in the waiting room, along with the patients who'd been hoping all weekend to hold off until their GP opened up on Monday, only to arrive pale and unwell in the early hours. Resus was filling. The early morning storm after a long dry spell ensured the roads were as slippery as ice and more than a couple of unfortunate motorists were paying the price.

'Isla.' Jayne nodded at Isla's apology. 'Could you give Heath a hand in the suture room? Then I'll bring you up to date with what's happening out here.'

If she was filled with trepidation at seeing Sav, the thought of seeing Heath filled her with horror, but, as she was new and appallingly late, Isla was hardly in a position to argue, so, forcing a professional stance, Isla walked into the suture room where Heath was stitching up a gentleman rather the worse for wear. The man was snoring loudly as Heath sutured his scalp.

'Do you want me to cut?' Isla offered.

'Please.' Heath nodded, barely looking up, but his darkening cheeks told Isla he was uncomfortable.

'There's eight waiting to be sutured, so a hand in here would be good.'

She didn't even attempt small talk, just snipped away with amazingly steady hands, irrigated wound after wound then dressed them as they worked their way through the list.

'Isla.' Washing the trolley when finally the list was over, she didn't even bother to look up. 'I really can't remember all that happened Saturday night.'

'Lucky you, then.' Green eyes fixed him to the spot.

'I'm sorry if I caused you and Sav any problems.'

'You didn't.'

'You're sure?' Heath checked, and Isla forced a smile.

'I'm sure.'

And she wasn't lying. Pushing the trolley

back against the wall, Isla ripped new paper off a roll and laid the table for the next patient, hating Heath for what he had done, but hating herself more for causing it.

Heath may have lit the rag, but it was she herself who'd gathered the wood.

'Isla.' Jayne grabbed her as she bustled past. Resus was screaming for another IVAC pump and Isla had finally resorted to running up to one of the wards and practically stealing one, but, from Isla's fairly blinkered view of Resus this morning, they really needed it, and desperate times called for desperate measures. 'Sav wants a word with you in his office.'

She'd been waiting all morning, the occasional glimpse of his busy head all she'd been privy to. Gone was the smiling, easygoing consultant, his unusually prickly mood setting the whole department on edge, but even though finally she would get to talk to him, work had to come first.

'I'll just give Nicole this pump—'

'I can do that.'

'It's on my way.' Isla shrugged. 'Surely Sav can wait two minutes. They need to start a streptokinase infusion for a confirmed AMI.'

'He's going to Theatre instead,' Jayne answered as Isla turned, practically wrestling the pump from her. 'So they don't need it now. I think you'd better go and see Sav.' Isla felt the beginning of a frown pucker her brow as Jayne pointed in the direction of Sav's office. She walked across the shiny floors of the department to Sav's untidy office.

And the frown stayed.

Stayed as she walked in and closed the door behind her.

Horrible truth began to dawn.

It was busy out there, so why was Sav in here?

Why was Sav holding his pen and staring at it, barely able to look her in the eye, directing her with his hand to a chair at his desk as if she were a patient...

Or a relative.

She could almost hear the kookaburras in the trees again, the sun blistering the back of her neck, when Sav finally looked up.

'This isn't about us, is it?' She gave a completely out-of-place laugh, crossed her legs then uncrossed them, fiddled with her name tag then shook her head
in dismay when finally Sav spoke.

'It's your father, Isla.'

'No.' She wasn't sure if she'd actually said it. Her mouth was moving, the word was there, but she didn't really hear it, just dragging in stuffy air, waiting for Sav to calm her, for Sav to step in and reassure her, to tell her it really wasn't that bad.

But he didn't.

'He's in Resus, Isla. He had an AMI an hour ago. Your mother's in there with him. She's been wonderful…' And on he went, telling her how Carmel had found him, given him aspirin while waiting for the ambulance to arrive. How she didn't—*they* didn't—want Isla to just walk in and see him in Resus. But she couldn't absorb it, couldn't really believe what she was hearing. 'Do you want me to take you to him?'

'In a moment.' She gave a brief nod, trying to compose herself, trying to silence the million questions whirring through her mind, to somehow come to terms with the next cruel blow that seemed to be aimed at her. But Sav was already standing, a moment more for Peter clearly not one he could guarantee.

'He's very sick, Isla. As soon as they can, they're taking him for an angio so we really ought to get over there.'

On legs that felt like jelly she walked through the department, vaguely aware of the sympathetic stares being cast in her direction from colleagues. Sav guided her, his hand loosely at her elbow, but when the resus doors slid open, when she saw her own father so grey and ill and frail on the resus bed, she felt his grip tighten, literally holding her up and guiding her forward.

'Dad.' Taking his hand, she held it, smiling as

his eyes flicked open. 'Try and rest now. You're going to be OK.'

'I'm sorry.' Peter shook his head against the pillow. 'You don't need this now, after all—'

'Dad, what I need is for you to get well, so rest. Please,' she added, but Peter's eyes turned to Sav.

'Look after her for me…'

'Rest,' Sav said gently. 'You need—'

'I need you to tell me you'll look after my girl!'

The silence seemed to go on for ever, broken only by the irregular bleeps from the monitor and Peter's ragged, hoarse breaths, until finally Sav stepped forward.

'I will *always* do my best for Isla.' Sav gripped his father-in-law's shoulders and stared him directly in the eye as he spoke. 'So stop worrying, Peter. Let us all just concentrate on getting you well.'

And he did his best.

Taking them through the appalling blur of the day, translating the doctors' long speeches into basic English, as much as for Isla as for Carmel, Isla's brain utterly unable to fathom much else.

'They needed to operate, they had no choice—he really needs this bypass,' Sav reiterated as the hours ticked by and they sat huddled on hard chairs outside the theatre waiting area, praying for no one to appear, finally understanding the saying that no news really was good news.

'He's too weak,' Isla said.

'Then you have to be strong,' Sav said resolutely. 'It's his only chance. The arteries are completely blocked.' He glanced down at his watch. 'I'll get the boys.'

'I'll ring Louise—' Isla started, but Sav shook his head.

'They need to hear it from one of us, Isla.'

'He's a good man.' Carmel smiled after Sav had gone. 'A very good man.'

'I know,' Isla whispered, watching his broad shoulders that bore so much weight moving down the corridor.

And later, much later, when she slid the key in the front door, directed her mother to the sofa and finally let out the breath she seemed to have been holding for ever, Sav proved it again.

'I should get home.' Carmel pushed the cheese on toast Sav had made around her plate, screwing her face up as she took a sip of the large brandy Sav had pushed into her hand. 'If the hospital rings—'

'You're staying here.' Sav's voice was insistent. 'I've made up the bed in the spare room and I'll ring the hospital in a moment to get an update and tell them where you are. You really can't be alone tonight.'

'Thank you.' Sitting, drooping with exhaustion on the bed in a nightdress she'd only ever worn on the maternity ward, Isla looked up as Sav came out of the *en suite*. His boxers and T-shirt were as out of place as her own attire. 'Thank you for not saying anything to Mum.'

'I'm not that much of a bastard.' He saw the

pain flash across her face and changed tack. 'Sleep, Isla.'

'I can't.'

'You have to.'

'What about tomorrow?' Her voice wobbled as she pulled back the sheets, nerves and ears on elastic, dreading the ringing of the phone as Sav flicked out the overhead light, leaving only the bedside lamp on as he climbed into the bed beside her. 'Sav, what about tomorrow?'

'We'll deal with it.'

'We?' Hope flared in her soul but died in an instant as she felt the shake of his head on the pillow next to her.

'Not that sort of we. What I said yesterday still stands.'

'So why are you here?' Isla asked, the bitterness evident in her voice. 'What was that little speech about to my father?'

'Because I love your family, love them as much as my own, and I know that now isn't the time for them to find out we have separated.'

'We haven't…'

'We have.' His voice was unequivocal. 'And I wasn't lying with what I said to your father. Whatever happens I will always do my best for you.'

'And leaving's best?'

'This is not the time to go over things. We really are over. However, for your parents' sake, we will delay telling them…'

'It won't work.' She shook her head, tears cascading down her cheeks. He didn't wipe them away. 'The boys will say something…'

'Have you told them?' He watched as her eyes screwed closed and she shook her head. 'Then we'll wait two weeks. I'll come home, we'll carry on as normally as we can, but once your father's better…'

'What if he's not?' Terrified eyes lifted to his.

'Then we all have to somehow pick up the pieces.'

CHAPTER TEN

IT SEEMED almost incongruous that at such an appallingly dark time happiness could even glimmer at the edges.

But it did.

Carmel taught Harry to tie his shoelaces, forcing Isla to cough up twenty dollars.

Luke lost two more teeth in one hit which, after Sav's extravagance, meant the poor tooth fairy was seriously in the red. Sav cooked paella thirteen nights in a row, somehow managing to juggle it all, somehow managing to be there, and one night, when Carmel was home, when the twins were asleep and life was almost normal, his hand reached out, pulling her towards him in the darkness, his hand slipping into the appalling nightdress, capturing her breast, his body spooning in behind her, loaded with desire. And even if he was asleep, even if the gesture wasn't conscious, it brought the first peace Isla had had for weeks. Lying next to him, being held by him, it took all the will-power she possessed not to turn around and kiss those full, sensual lips, not to take full advantage of the sudden intimacy. And even though she knew, just knew he would reciprocate, Isla couldn't bear to see the regret in his eyes the next morning…

The gang in Emergency, aware of part of Isla's plight, decided to put the usual initiation period for a newcomer on hold and embrace her fully into the clique, waving her into Resus if anything interesting came in, adding her to the coffee and cake roster, even letting her take every last patient—even if she hadn't so much as lain eyes on them up till then—up to CCU so she could grab a quick five minutes with her father.

'You're looking good, Dad,' Isla commented one day, peeling a bruising banana and grinning at the amazingly pink face that smiled back at her. She hoped Sav could see it as clearly as she could. Yes, Peter missed Casey, mourned him, yearned for him, but it hadn't just been his grandson's death that had brought him here, he'd been ill all along. 'They'll be kicking you out soon.'

'Tomorrow!' Grinning from ear to ear, selecting a banana of his own, Peter didn't notice the smile disappear from his daughter's face. 'The doc just came round and told me that if I can walk to the lift and back this afternoon and there's no funny stuff with my heart between now and the next ward round, I can go home.'

And because they were stretched, because coronary-care beds were as rare as hen's teeth, Peter didn't make it to the next ward round. In fact, he barely made it to the lift before his bed was stripped and made up for the next occupant. Instead, he sat in his own chair, bemoaning the boiled, saltless chicken Carmel had lovingly prepared for him as Isla reeled at the speed of it all, reeled not only that her father, so sick, so fragile, was home but that her temporary crutch was gone, that injury time was well and truly over now and a penalty shoot-out was waiting.

'What are you doing?' Walking into the bedroom, she stiffened as Sav zipped up a toiletry bag.

'The same as last time, only this time it's for good.'

One-nil to Sav.

'I thought you said you'd wait—'

'And I did wait.' Plunging the bag into a suit cover, he finally looked at her. 'Your dad's fine. We can't baby him for ever.'

'I'm not babying him. He's just got out of hospital. How on earth do you think this news will affect him? How the hell—?'

'Hopefully he'll find out a little more gently that our marriage is over than I did.'

Two-nil to Sav.

'Mummy.' A loud rap on the door had them both on high alert, Sav stiff and awkward as Harry and Luke walked in.

'What's the problem, guys?' Sav's voice was a poor attempt at normality as Luke held up his hand.

'Luke's got a blister.'

'Come here.' Ignoring the awful atmosphere, Isla attempted to focus on her son, probing the white blister on his hand. 'When did this happen?'

'Dunno.' Luke shrugged.

'She's getting a pin.' Harry grinned as Isla headed for the door.

'Let me see.' Taking his son's hand, Sav looked at it closely. 'It's a simple blister. All it needs is a sticking plaster.'

'It needs to be lanced,' Isla snarled through gritted teeth.

'You don't disturb blisters.' For the sake of the boys Sav's voice was even, but his eyes were dark as he eyed her across the room. 'A blister is nature's way of—'

'In an ideal world perhaps, but he's a seven-year-old boy.' Isla's lips were white. 'The sticking plaster will come off by the morning, he'll burst the blister. It's better to do it this way.'

'Leave it,' Sav insisted.

'To fester?' Isla looked up sharply and suddenly they weren't talking about a tiny blister. 'Cover it up and hope that it heals?'

'Better than exposing a raw wound,' Sav bit back.

'So who's right?' Luke looked up expectantly, his blue eyes swivelling from one to the other.

'The doctor or the nurse?' Harry added, just to splash another dollop of fuel on the fire.

'I'll get a sticking plaster.' Isla stood up and brushed past him. 'Though the way this house runs, I'm surprised we've got any left.'

'Can we read?' Happy with his plaster, Luke jumped off the bed. 'Just for five minutes?'

'It's time you were asleep,' Sav's voice was suddenly thick. He grabbed the boys in a huge hug and kissed them hard.

'Please, Dad?'

'No.' His eyes caught on the book Harry was holding, the bright cut-out shapes adorning the cover, a happy teddy smiling in the middle. 'What are you doing, reading that?' He took the book, turned it over in his hand. 'You're way past this. Why are you getting baby books from the library?'

'We like them.' Harry swallowed hard, staring nervously at Isla, his eyes sending a silent plea for help.

'Sav.' Isla's voice was a croak. 'Leave it.'

'But this is for a four-year-old.'

'Go to bed, boys.' Retrieving the book, she handed it to Harry, kissed them both and watched as they scampered down the hall.

'Isla, don't undermine me like that. The boys are seven. They should be—'

'They read to Casey.' She watched his face slip as the pin stuck in, as she lanced the wound that had festered too long, saw the chasm of despair in his eyes as maybe, just maybe the truth hit home. 'Every week they choose books from the library so they can read Casey a story at night.

'But, I guess, like me, they just weren't able to tell you.'

CHAPTER ELEVEN

WITH crisis came change.

Isla didn't know where she'd heard it, but she believed it.

Believed it enough to drag herself out of bed the next morning and pull on her uniform, to drop the kids at the eternally patient Louise's and drive to work.

Things *had* to change.

And, for better or worse, now they would. Sav had been wonderful for the last two weeks, supporting her family, taking over the strain of the boys, being there for her as he always had been in a physical sense. But the distance was evident, the incident with the library book proof, if ever Isla had needed it, that they simply couldn't go on like this. For the boys' sake more than hers.

Isla hadn't really expected to see Sav straight off, had consoled herself she'd have an hour or so of grace before he arrived at work, but she found him huddled on a stool in the nurses' station, talking into the phone and doodling on a pad, dressed in baggy theatre blues and an old white coat, dark and brooding, as if he were sitting in a gale-force storm. There was absolutely no way of avoiding him and Isla took a deep breath and tried to breeze into the gathering throng of early shift nurses, determined to greet him with a professional 'Good morning' if he deigned to look at her. But Sav had other ideas and pointedly didn't look up when she came over to the nurses' station. But he managed a smile for Jayne as she placed a steaming cup of coffee in front of him.

'I figured he deserves it,' Jayne said, catching Isla looking over. 'Seeing that he's been here since three. But, then, you already know that.'

Her unintentional twist of the knife had Sav's

eyes jerk up. Isla felt herself staring back, her stance almost defiant, daring him, *daring him* to do this—to take the first step, tell the first person, take a pin to the balloon and burst it all right there and then. But clearly seven-fifteen a.m. in front of a gathering crowd wasn't quite the time, and it was Sav who broke the moment, Sav who dragged his eyes away and Isla finally let out the breath she had inadvertently been holding.

Wherever Sav had been last night, it didn't appear to have had a razor. His usually clean-shaven face was peppered with dark early morning stubble, his eyes dark holes in his tense face. He hadn't dived into the staff showers yet, which with any other human Isla could think of would have been a turn-off. But with Sav it had the opposite effect on her. His heavy male scent was accentuated now, and at the most ridiculous, inappropriate, pathetically inexcusable time Isla felt weak at the knees with lust, longing to push aside all the hell that was holding them apart, to make everyone some-

how disappear and place her hands on those tired broad shoulders, to run her fingers through that tousled hair, to kiss away all the pain and hurt in
his strained face.

'Isla?'

Jayne's voice made her jump and she stared over at the slightly bemused, impatient crowd gathered outside cubicle one, waiting to start. Beating back a blush, she made her way over and forced herself to focus as handover proceeded.

But work soon took over, the real world soon caught up as Isla submerged herself in other people's problems, almost relieved to find out that, as bad as her world seemed right now, there were a lot of people worse off.

'Ivy!' Pulling open the curtain, Isla stared at the familiar face of her first *real* patient in seven years. She'd recognized her name as soon as the night nurse had said it, and had listened with growing sadness when she'd heard how Ivy had been discharged only the previous day and had fallen again, this time thankfully only fracturing her nose.

And fracturing her spirit, Isla thought as the once beady eyes didn't look up. Ivy's face was swathed in gauze and purple bruises were already spreading under her eyes.

'What happened?'

'Ivy fell.' Amy didn't look great this morning either as she sat beside her sister, the make-up replaced with tired, red-rimmed eyes, the smart hair almost as wild and woolly as her sister's. 'I wanted her to come home to us, but Ivy insisted, as she always does, that she was fine—didn't even want the supper I brought over for her. I heard a crash around four this morning.'

'Oh, Ivy.' Isla pulled up a chair. 'What did the doctor say?'

'That I can't go home,' Ivy whispered. 'That I'm not capable—'

'He didn't,' Amy interjected. 'The doctor said that you need more help, more support, which I'm prepared to give. You can come and live with me.'

'If I give up drinking.' Ivy stared angrily at her sister, and when Amy didn't deny it she turned to Isla. 'I'm eighty-two years old, for goodness' sake, what's the point? Why should I deny myself my one pleasure?'

'It's not a pleasure any more, though, Ivy.' Sav's thick accent had Isla's cheeks flaming as he pulled open the curtain and walked in. 'You've only been home from hospital one night and already you're back. With the right help and support, you can give up drinking and have a full—'

'I have a full life,' Ivy interrupted, a flash of the feisty woman Isla had witnessed a few weeks ago emerging. 'Much fuller than I'd have strapped to a rocking chair in Amy's house, with a hundred grandchildren running around, and Amy telling me how lucky I am to have her.'

'It wouldn't be like that,' Amy said and Sav turned to her.

'Would you excuse us?' Sav flashed a very

nice, very kind smile to Amy. 'Maybe you could use a coffee?'

Pulling up a chair as Amy left, Sav paused for a long moment before talking. 'I've been on the phone to Eden Lodge—'

'The madhouse?' Ivy barked, but Sav shook his head.

'No, it's a rehabilitation unit. It'll mean staying there for a few weeks and learning how to live life without alcohol. If you're prepared to give it a go, they're ready to have you. I've spent the last two hours on the telephone, convincing them to let you jump the queue, assuring them that you're a good candidate for rehabilitation.'

'Well, you've been wasting your time. There's nothing about me that needs rehabilitating. A bit of peace and quiet is all I need!'

'You need support,' Sav said firmly, and Ivy gave a loud snort.

'What am I supposed to do? Shuffle off to AA meetings on my Zimmer frame? You'll have me giving up salt next and taking aerobics classes.'

'You have a family that loves you, Ivy, a family that wants you to join them…'

'Well, I don't want to join them. Bloody kids everywhere.'

'You don't like children?'

'I don't like their noise. I'd rather be alone.'

'With your memories?' Sav said softly, but then his voice changed. 'Or with your vodka?'

'What would you know?' Ivy stared angrily back at him. 'What would you know about grief? I bet you've got a lovely little wife waiting for you at home, a houseful of kids—'

'Ivy.' It was Isla interrupting now, Isla feeling that, as much as it was par for the course in this line of work, things really were getting too personal. 'These sorts of places don't come up very often. Now, you have to make a choice—either take the help that Dr Ramirez's offering or—'

'Or what?' Ivy shouted. 'You'll send me anyway?'

'Not at all.' Isla shook her head. 'You can go home now. Dr Ramirez will arrange an outpatient appointment with ENT to assess your nose once the swelling goes down and I'll call the social worker and try to arrange meals on wheels…'

'Amy does my meals.'

'No.' Sav stood up. 'Amy has her own life, one that you're welcome to join, but she's not going to prop you up any more, Ivy. She's not going to provide your meals and go to bed at night with one ear open in case you fall. Quite simply, she can't do it any more, can't sit by and watch you destroy your life. So if you don't go into rehab, next Sunday she's flying to Queensland to see some of her grandchildren.'

'Leaving me?' Ivy roared.

'Perhaps.' Sav shrugged. 'Or perhaps you'll be in Eden Lodge, getting yourself sorted, preparing yourself for a wonderful life that's waiting for you if only you'll let it in.'

'How can it be wonderful without Eddie?'

For a second Isla felt as if she were looking into Sav's eyes, the pain, the agony so clearly visible in Ivy's. 'Everyone says I should be over it…'

'You'll never get over it,' Isla said softly. 'You'll never have a day when you don't miss him, Ivy, but with the right help, if you let in the people around you who love you, in a little while you'll slowly start to learn to live with the pain without drowning in it. Life can still be good.'

Maybe there was something in Isla's voice that told Ivy she was speaking from the heart, that she wasn't just another nurse who had read the books, but someone who possibly understood. After a long silence the old lady nodded, and Isla felt a sting of tears in her eyes as she took the first brave step. Isla's heart tripped to a stop as she felt Sav's warm hand close over her shoulder, giving a tiny squeeze, though of what she didn't know. Encouragement? Support?

Understanding?

'Can I tell Eden Lodge that you're coming?' Sav's voice was thick with emotion, his hand still on Isla's shoulder.

'When?'

'Today.'

'How will I get there?'

'In an ambulance. It might take a while to organize. You'll need a nurse escort.'

'Can Isla come with me?'

Sav hesitated, and with good reason. An Emergency trained RN, even if she was a relative newcomer, was a rather essential commodity, and under normal circumstances the escort would have been arranged from Outpatients or the hospital bank. But a final tiny squeeze before he removed his hand from Isla's shoulder told her that Sav understood the old lady's fears, that it wasn't all about budgets and numbers but about people.

'I'll do my best.'

Which was enough.

An ambulance came within the hour, and Isla smiled at Ted and Doug as they loaded the old lady into the ambulance chair, chatting amicably with her, even teasing her as she made them wait while she put on her lipstick.

'Eden Lodge won't know what's hit them,' Sav said as Isla collected the X-rays and letter he had written. He looked more like the old Sav now. He was dressed in a French navy suit, his white shirt accentuating his swarthy skin and that delicious strong jaw, clean shaven now and splashed with way too much of the heady aftershave Isla bought him each Father's Day, every bit the dashing consultant, ready to deliver the weekly doctor's lecture. But for a moment he was Sav, and she was Isla. 'You did well with her.' The smile slipped from his face, his expression suddenly serious. 'You really got through to her.'

'If only it was always so easy.' Her voice was soft, her eyes holding his. 'I don't think it was all me, Sav. I guess Ivy was just ready for change.'

She could see the grooves around his eyes, lines that hadn't been there eighteen months ago, flecks of grey fanning his sideburns, and ached to reach out, to capture that proud tired face in her hands. But it wasn't the place, and it certainly wasn't the time.

Sav had to come to her.

'Have you told the boys about what's happened?'

Isla shook her head. 'I thought it should come from both of us.'

And then he said it, the three little words she had waited for ever to hear—not 'I love you' because that had never been in doubt, but three little words that had been absent for so long now.

'Can we talk?'

'Isla, ready for the off?' Ted was coming up behind her, completely unaware of what he was interrupting, which was as it should be, of course, but even though it was work, even though it was a busy Monday in Emergency, some things simply couldn't wait.

'About?' Isla's eyes were on Sav.

'Us,' Sav said, his eyes screwing closed for a tiny fraction. 'Casey.'

'You know we can.' Clutching the notes to her chest, she managed a brave smile, her heart swelling inside, that this difficult proud man could drag them back from the brink more a comfort than she could have ever imagined. 'I have to go.'

She could feel his eyes burning into her as she stepped through the sliding doors of the ambulance entrance, turned around for one quick wave and smiled back at him. As she settled Ivy, strapped in her seat belt and chatted to the paramedics, Sav's face appeared at the door. 'You forgot the ENT outpatient appointment.'

'Thanks.' The look that flashed between them was as intense, as intimate, as close as a look could be.

As Ted closed the ambulance door, as they indicated and pulled out of the bay, Sav knew he should have headed back in, heaven knows there was enough waiting for him to do, but a shiver of foreboding ran through him as the ambulance slipped from view into the busy morning traffic.

There was so much that needed to be said.

Surely there was still time.

'Ivy!' Grabbing the bottle, Isla shook her head, furious with herself for chatting too long to Ted and not noticing Ivy sneak a bottle out of her handbag. 'You can't have a drink.'

'Just one,' Ivy moaned. 'One last one.'

'They won't take you if you smell of alcohol,' Isla scolded, suppressing a smile as Ted shot her a wink. 'You're supposed to be trying to give up.'

'And I will, once I get there,' Ivy huffed.

'Well, no time like the present. We're here now.' Ted grinned as the ambulance pulled up in the driveway of a small hospital-like building. 'Your new home for the next few weeks.'

'Doesn't look much like a home,' Ivy moaned, as they wheeled her into the foyer. 'It looks more like an institution if you ask me.' She gave a low, dry laugh. 'But, then, why would anyone care what I think? I'm just the old coot.'

'Just try and make the best of it,' Isla soothed, willing Ivy to be quiet as a rather bossy-looking woman made her way over.

'Mrs Dullard?' She shook the reluctant patient's hand. 'I'm Noelene, the unit manager.'

'This is Ivy,' Isla ventured, praying the manager would force a smile so that Ivy wouldn't demand to be let out at the first hurdle.

'And I assume this is Ivy's vodka?' Noelene said knowingly, taking the bottle Isla was clutching.

'Hoping for a quick final belt in the ambulance before you got here, were you?'

'Do you blame me?' Ivy answered cheekily, but Noelene had an answer.

'Completely, Ivy.

'Right, Martha will take you through to the admission room and go through your bag and coat with you, just to check you haven't brought any more little surprises, and then we'll get the admitting doctor down to see you.'

'Good luck, Ivy.' Isla gave her a quick hug before Ted wheeled Ivy off. 'Remember, these people are here to help you.'

'Kill me more like,' Ivy shouted over her shoulder, leaving Isla alone with the manager.

'Poor old thing,' Isla ventured as Noelene read through Sav's admission letter. 'She lost her husband.'

'Twenty years ago,' Noelene pointed out. 'And a "poor old thing" is how Ivy considers herself when, in fact, she's actually bloody lucky. She's got a sister who's willing to take her, which is more than most people have.'

'She's really very sweet.'

'And very manipulative.' Noelene looked up from the letter. 'She's already got you wrapped around her little finger.'

'I guess,' Isla admitted, with a wry smile. 'Do you think she'll make it?'

'That's up to Ivy.' Noelene gave a tight shrug, then her face softened for a fleeting moment. 'She's a tough old boot, but she's at least got her pride and a bit of fight left in her. It's nice that she takes care of her appearance.'

'Do you think?' Isla's eyes widened, thinking of the wild grey hair and tatty old coat.

'She still puts on her lipstick, still manages to make a bit of an effort—it's a good sign. The doctor will start her on an alcohol withdrawal regime. We'll give her Valium to get her through the first few days, given her age and everything, and there will be lots of counselling and support for her from the team, but at the end of the day it's Ivy's choice. All we can do is give her a chance—it's up to Ivy whether she takes it.'

'Any chance of a cuppa, Noelene?' Doug and Ted were back from admissions. And for the first time since Isla had met her, Noelene actually bordered on approachable, her stern face breaking into a semblance of a smile, a hint of a blush dusting her cheeks.

'Of course, Dougie. How about you two?'

'Not for me,' Ted said. 'I've got me Thermos

in the ambulance, and some nice biscuits. Fancy a yarn and a cuppa while I tidy up the van, Isla?'

'Sounds great,' Isla said, leaving the blushing duo to it.

'Dougie lives for call-outs to Eden Lodge,' Ted said, pouring steaming coffee into a cup and handing it to Isla.

'Is that why we got an ambulance so quickly?' Isla asked with a laugh and Ted nodded.

'He almost put on the blue lights. They've been carrying on like that for years now. Dougie's just never had the courage to ask her out.'

'Well, he should.' Isla took a sip of her hot sweet brew. 'Did you see the way she blushed? They look made for each other.'

'Like you and Sav.' Ted took a noisy slurp of his coffee and thankfully didn't notice the tiny wince on Isla's face. 'He's a great guy.'

'I know,' Isla admitted, because, quite simply, he was, but Ted looked up.

'I know, you know.' He looked at her thought-fully. 'Must be hard on you both.'

'It has been,' Isla admitted slowly, frowning as Ted carried on talking.

'I know when my Bess died I was like Ivy there for a while. Too happy to get home and pour a large whisky.'

'But you got through it. I mean, you seem happy now.'

Ted shrugged. 'I am happy, but I tell you what, Isla, sometimes it's nice to get home and let the mask slip. I know Sav always seems happy and that, but I reckon it's the same for him, huh? Must be good for him to get home and just be himself.'

He didn't see her frown, didn't see her sit staring into her coffee as the radio on the dash-board crackled into life.

And suddenly she understood.

No one was wrong and no one was right ei-ther.

It was just grief.

The hard long road of grief that you had to

walk for the most part alone, but sometimes every now and then you could, if you read the signs carefully, meet up along the way then hopefully, at some stage, arrive back home together.

Tonight they'd be together.

Tonight they'd stop for a while and find out how the other one was doing.

Be there for each other, compromise for each other and hopefully, hopefully take some steps together.

'We've got a call-out.' Ted sounded the horn as Isla hastily threw out the last of the coffee and packed up the remains of their break. 'Priority one,' Ted shouted as Dougie jumped into the driver's seat. 'Heart-attack victim at the shopping centre in the high street. There's a doctor in attendance, giving BLS.' All this was said as the ambulance screeched out of the driveway, sirens and lights blaring, and Isla sat on the stretcher in the back of the ambulance and clipped on her lap belt, a bubble of excitement welling inside as the ambulance raced through the morning traffic on its way to someone in need. It was like riding a roller-coaster as Doug accelerated and braked. Her fingers were white as she gripped the underside of the stretcher beneath her, eyeing the LifePak defibrillator, thrilled that she was going to be an active part of this.

Because emergency nurses lived for this. Each and every one surely at some time considered joining the paramedics—being first at the scene, making life-and-death decisions with very little back-up.

High on adrenaline, her heart thumping with excitement, Isla sucked in her breath as the ambulance jolted. She felt the surge as Doug slammed on the brakes, but somewhere it all went wrong. Just as the vehicle should have accelerated again, she felt the vehicle tip, the screech of brakes coupled with a horrible lurch as Ted let out a shout. She saw the flash of a cyclist darting across the road and she thought she should be screaming, but she was trying too hard just to hold on, could feel her upper body hurtling from one side to the other, her cheek slamming against cold metal over and over as the sound of metal meeting concrete ripped through her ears. Her hands flailed wildly, trying to buffer herself, trying to somehow cling on, as glass popped around her, one final, lucid stream of thought as she spun like a rag doll in a tumble-dryer as the ambulance finally tipped on its side and skidded to a noisy halt.

Sav.

Harry.

Luke.

Casey.

They all thundered into her mind with more impact than the car that was slamming into the wreckage. And then it was Sav all over again. Did he know how much she loved him?

CHAPTER TWELVE

'CAN I have a word, Heath?'

Sav frowned as Jayne popped her head around the door. The hours between ten and eleven on a Monday morning were sacred, used exclusively for the weekly doctor's lecture. Only the most serious of emergencies merited an interruption.

'Problem?' Sav checked.

'Nothing Heath can't deal with,' Jayne said lightly—too lightly, Sav thought, his forehead creasing into a frown as Heath mumbled his apologies and ducked out. And suddenly the merits of intra-osseous infusions as opposed to IV cutdown didn't seem to matter very much to anyone, his audience lost for good now as again Jayne's head appeared around the door.

'We've had an alert from Ambulance Control, guys. Multi-vehicle pile-up, with multiple injuries. We're sending out the squad.' Jayne nodded to Martin Elmes, the senior consultant, just back from his extended leave. 'We haven't got an estimated time of arrival yet, I just thought I should let you all know.'

'I'm down for the squad today,' Sav pointed out, the lecture forgotten as he started to cross the room. 'Why did you call Heath out?'

'Because he needs the experience,' Jayne snapped uncharacteristically, especially given the fact they were in a room full of doctors. 'Give him his head, would you, Sav? He hasn't been out with the squad for ages.

'Martin, can I borrow you for a moment?' she added.

Suddenly Sav felt as if he'd been kicked in the stomach, that niggling sense of foreboding, which had stayed with him since he'd said goodbye to Isla, increasing now. He tried to reason it out, to rationalize the fears that were pinging into his mind at an appalling rate, to take deep breaths and stay in control, to reassure himself that everything was OK.

But if everything was OK, why wasn't anybody looking at him? Why, as he walked through the department, did everyone seem to disappear, suddenly too busy to look up and smile? There wasn't one single request for his attention, not a single person meeting his eyes as he strode out to the entrance.

'I'm going out with the squad,' he barked, heading for the equipment cupboard, just in time to see Heath pulling on his backpack as he darted outside to the waiting ambulance. Lights and sirens were blazing, Sav's voice as he called his colleague drowned out in the noise. But for some reason Heath stopped, shouted something to the waiting ambos and headed back.

'I'm taking Sav.'

'No!' Jayne's normally laid-back voice was perhaps the most assertive Sav had heard it outside the resus room. Even Martin Elmes was joining in the chorus, pulling Sav back with one hand and waving Heath on.

'I'm taking Sav,' Heath said again, more loudly this time, his decision firmly made. Sav didn't need to be asked twice. Even if Heath had taken back his offer, it would have been too late. Already he was jumping into the ambulance, slamming the door, bile churning in his gut as his worst fears appeared to be being confirmed. He turned to face the man who right now he maybe should have hated most in the world, but right now really needed.

'What the hell's going on, Heath?'

'I'm not sure…' Heath started, but Sav waved the prevarication away.

'I need to know now!' Sav was shouting to be heard above the sirens as the ambulance tore out of the bay.

'One of the vehicles in the accident may be an ambulance!' Heath waited a second before continuing, watching as Sav's eyes widened in horror, his face paling, clenching his fists against his temples. 'Apparently the vehicle that's called for assistance has a nurse escort on board.'

'Isla?' His voice was a hoarse whisper and Heath didn't hear it, just watched his colleague's pale lips form the two syllables.

'We don't know for sure. There's a switch on the console of the ambulance, like a panic button. That's gone off. They could just be assisting at an accident. We don't know for sure that they're involved…'

'Bull!' Sav shook his head, gulping in air, nausea so vile he could taste it. 'They don't press that button just for assistance—that button's only used if the crew's in trouble. It gridlocks the system—every ambulance, every police car races to the scene. You know that,' he said, his voice rising. *'You know that!'*

'Sav!' It was Heath shouting now, his voice a mental slap to Sav's pale cheek. 'Till we get there we won't know anything! Now, you know as well as I do that you shouldn't be here, that a family member is the last thing we need at a scene like this—'

'I *have* to be there,' Sav interrupted fiercely, and Heath nodded.

'I know. But, Sav, you have to let me go in there first, I mean that. I'm going to go in and assess and I'll—'

'I'm going in with you.'

'No!' Heath's voice was equally firm. 'I'm the doctor in charge here, Sav! This is my callout and you are not going in there until I say so. Now, if I can't trust you to wait for me, I'll tell them up front to turn around…' He held Sav's savage glare. 'I'll tell them that there's a chance it's your wife at the scene and to send out another team from another hospital.'

'And how much time will that waste?' Sav growled.

'Too much,' Heath snapped. 'So you're going to sit tight till I call you.'

Which was an impossible ask, so, instead of sitting tight, he stood as the ambulance slowed down, closed his eyes in a second of silent prayer as the police waved them through, his heart stilling as he eyed the mangled wreckage of an ambulance, lying like a discarded toy on its side, a car impacted into its rear rendering access difficult, smoke pouring out the front as firefighters applied foam. It was like watching a horror movie, like living a nightmare all over again. He could almost smell his own fear, feel appalling memories he'd sworn never to relive flashing in as his heart tripped into life again, pumping loudly in his temples. He knew, just knew that Isla was in there.

That Isla, his Isla whom he'd sworn to protect, had promised to love and make happy, was trapped in the same hell he'd once witnessed.

'Stay here,' Heath warned, as Sav lifted the backpack containing lifesaving equipment onto Heath's shoulders.

'I need to be with her.' Sav gripped his arm, stared into his colleague's eyes and saw something that hadn't been there for ages—integrity? Honour? He couldn't quite place it, but something told him that the old Heath was back, that finally once more he could trust him. 'Even if she's—'

'I'll call for you.' They were waiting for the all-clear, for the firefighters to give the thumbs-up and let them in. 'I'm sorry, Sav, not just for this, but for what happened the other night…'

'Later,' Sav said through chattering teeth. 'We can deal with all of that later. Like it or not, right now both Isla and I need you.'

CHAPTER THIRTEEN

SHE glimpsed his hell.

Maybe for the first time Isla understood why Sav didn't want to talk about it.

The appalling sound of silence as the world slowly came into focus. The ear-splitting noises that had surrounded her as she'd plunged into unconsciousness way more palatable than the noises that were starting to drift in now—the treacherous sound of an obstructed airway, laboured, slow breaths that demanded her assistance, but even as Isla went to move she knew it would be futile. She felt the heavy weight of metal on her chest before she registered the pain and understood that she was trapped.

'Isla?' She could hear Ted's gruff voice in the darkness.

'Ted!' It was more a gasp than a word, every breath a supreme effort as the mangled stretcher that pinned her seemed to grip tighter, her one free hand working out the structure as her eyes struggled to focus. 'Ted?' She said it louder, more forcibly this time.

'It's OK, Isla. I've hit the panic button. Help's coming.'

It had to be coming, Isla reasoned. They were in the middle of a busy street, people would be jamming the phone lines calling for help. But why wasn't it here? Why wasn't someone helping?

'Doug?' With mounting panic she listened to his laboured breathing, pushed at the stretcher with her hands, desperately trying to budge it, to move legs she couldn't even feel, to go and render some desperately needed assistance. 'Ted, you have to do something. I can't, I'm trapped. Doug's airway's blocked, he needs—'

'I can't!' His two tortured words said it all, and Isla's eyes screwed closed as Ted spoke on. 'I can't get over to him. My legs are pinned.'

'OK.' Isla gulped in air, every breath an agony in itself, tried to keep her voice calm. 'It's OK, Ted. I can hear sirens. They'll help Dougie. You just have to stay still, you could have hurt your neck…'

'But Dougie needs help now! I can't just sit here and listen to him die. Where the hell is everyone?' It was Ted that needed reassurance now, Ted that needed the support as his colleague lay dying a few feet away. 'Why the hell aren't they doing anything?'

'They'll be here,' Isla said with more conviction than she felt, watching the eerie glow from the emergency vehicle's blue lights circling around her, listening to the shouts from outside, hearing the sirens and screaming and crying growing louder, but not loud enough to drown out the silence from Doug.

'Dougie!' Ted was shouting now, shouting and crying at the same time, and Isla could feel her own tears stinging her raw cheeks as Ted called louder. 'Dougie, mate, hang in there.'

And then more urgently. 'Isla, he's not breathing. I can't hear him breathing!'

It was the longest three minutes of her life.

Praying, waiting for help to arrive, for someone—anyone—to appear, to give Dougie the help he so desperately needed. It was sheer torture to lie in the remains of a fully stocked ambulance, to know that you were capable, more than capable of dealing with it, yet being able to do nothing.

Absolutely nothing.

'He's gone.' Ted's choked voice ended the vigil, and Isla nodded, more scared than she had ever been in her life. But the shot of adrenaline that had forced her into alertness was wearing off now, and as her eyes grew heavier, Isla knew she should struggle to keep them open, should fight to stay awake, fight the injuries that were dragging her towards oblivion, but right now the sweet release of unconsciousness was a far more palatable option.

'We're in!' A loud shout snapped her back to consciousness, her hand shooting over her eyes as a bright torch shone directly down at her. 'It's OK, love.' She couldn't see the face of the person that was talking, but the voice was strong and steady and in control, and Isla felt herself relax a notch. 'I'm Mike. I'm the chief firefighter, co-ordinating the rescue. We're going to get you out just as soon as we can. Can you tell me your name?'

'Isla.'

'Anyone else?' The light was flashing around the vehicle now, taking in every detail, working out the casualties, their positions and the wreckage that encased them, but all the time keeping up what seemed like almost idle chatter.

'Ted,' Isla gasped.

'I'm here,' Ted responded. 'Don't worry about me, just get Isla out.'

'We will,' Mike assured him. 'Is there anyone else in here?'

'Dougie, he's the driver,' Ted answered, his voice flat as the torch flashed towards his colleague. 'You're too late.'

'Did you have any passengers?' Mike asked and maybe his lack of acknowledgement for Dougie sounded callous, but right now his main priority was to look after the living. Mourning the loss of a fellow emergency worker would come later. Isla and Ted thankfully didn't know the full extent of the damage, that a car was sandwiching them against a set of traffic lights, that an engine fire had almost taken hold, and with the combination of oxygen tanks and fuel a massive explosion had just been averted. 'OK, guys, I'm going to get a paramedic and doctor in to you now, then we're going to get the side off the vehicle— which is going to make one helluva noise, but once we've done that we'll be able to get some of this wreckage away and get you both out.'

'Which doctor?' Isla asked, but Mike wasn't listening. His shadow disappeared, her question apparently irrelevant, but the thought of Sav seeing her unprepared, of him thinking this was just another accident and then seeing her trapped there, was causing Isla more angst than the metal pressing down on her. 'Which doctor, Mike?'

'This one!' It was the second last voice she wanted to hear.

A—Isla thought as her nightmare plunged from horrific into dire, she hated him.

B—from what she'd seen so far, Heath wasn't the greatest doctor in the world.

And most importantly…

C—if Heath was here, did Sav know?

'Sav?' It was her first question as Heath climbed through the shattered window and made his way over slowly, followed by a paramedic who moved directly towards where Ted lay trapped.

'Sav knows.' Heath was beside her now, picking up her wrist and feeling the flickering pulse for a moment, then pulling out a cervical collar and starting to apply it.

'My neck's fine.'

'Save your breath, Ramirez,' Heath said, but she could hear a hint of kindness behind his voice. Once her neck was stabilized and an oxygen mask put on to deliver oxygen, he squeezed her arm just above the wrist in an attempt to bring up a vein. 'I brought Sav with me—figured you could use a bit of diversion.

'Sharp scratch coming,' he added needlessly, because a sting in the back of her hand was the least of her problems. 'Sav's outside. As soon as I've got you stable, I'll let him in.'

'Why did it take so long for help to come?' Her words were muffled under the mask and she pulled it off. 'Why did it take so long?'

'The engine was smoking,' Heath replied, replacing the mask, but again Isla pulled it off with her free hand.

'I want nasal prongs.'

'You need oxygen,' Heath insisted.

'Then I'll breathe through my nose. I need to talk, Heath.'

'Who was it that said nurses make the worst patients?' But amazingly he complied, replacing the mask with prongs, watching her oxygen saturation while he carried on talking. Isla dragged in the air through her nose, determined not to be smothered with a mask as he connected IV fluids and hung them on a hook, giving a wry smile as he did so. The IV hook was the one thing in the ambulance that was where it was supposed to be. 'The first on the scene dealt with the car that went into you—they couldn't get to the ambulance.'

Isla's voice wobbled as the full magnitude of the accident started to hit home. 'Is it a family? Are there children?'

'I don't know,' Heath answered, and Isla had no choice but to believe him. 'You're my patient, Isla, you're the only one I'm worried about right now, and given that you're my boss's wife, I'm going to make damn sure you're OK.'

'Is Sav OK?'

'Worry about yourself for now, Isla.' He was examining her now as best he could with the snarl of metal around her. 'Where does it hurt most?'

'My chest.'

'How are your legs?'

'OK, I think.'

He shone a torch over down to her feet. 'Wiggle your toes.'

'I am.' She snapped a nervous look up at him. 'Aren't I?'

'You are!' He gave a relieved smile and Isla even managed a small one back as Heath pulled on his stethoscope, trying to listen to her chest, but the mangled stretcher allowed only very limited access. 'Poor air entry, but with a stretcher on your chest you've got a good excuse.'

He was good, Isla had to hand it to him. Somehow his flip remarks almost reassured her, but even if she'd been away from nursing for an age, some things stayed with you for ever, and the look of controlled urgency in Heath's eyes needed no translation.

This was serious.

'How's my blood pressure?' Isla asked, as Heath pumped the cuff over and over.

'Not bad.'

'In my boots, then.'

'How's the pain?'

She hesitated, but only for a second. 'Bad.'

He was listening to the top of her chest again, trying to slip the stethoscope down further, but the tight band of metal around her chest prevented him.

'Tell me, Heath,' Isla insisted. 'What's going on?'

'I'm not sure,' Heath said finally, but realizing she needed a small dose of truth he relented slightly, understanding she was an emergency nurse, that platitudes would do nothing to reassure her, but the truth wasn't particularly palatable either. 'Your air entry on the right is markedly reduced. It could be bad bruising, the pressure of the stretcher…'

'Or?' He didn't answer so Isla did it for him. 'I could have punctured my lung. I could have a pneumothorax or, worse, a haemopneumothorax. Shouldn't you put in a chest drain?' Panic was rising in her now and Heath moved quickly to soothe her.

'Don't go there, Isla. Right now, I can't get in

to listen properly to your chest, let alone put a chest tube in, but you're holding your oxygen saturation with the oxygen. For now we'll give you fluids and oxygen and in the meantime I'll get all the equipment ready. We'll know more when we move the stretcher,' Heath said firmly.

Despite his assured tones Isla felt anything but reassured. If the stretcher had punctured her lung, it would be as dangerous as removing a knife from a stab wound once the stretcher was lifted. She could bleed out quickly. Even the rapid insertion of a chest tube and a massive transfusion of blood might not be enough to save her.

'I'm going to give you something for the pain, something to settle you before they lift the roof.'

She would have nodded but the hard collar prevented it.

'Any allergies?'

'Strawberries.'

'Well, luckily we're in short supply of strawberries at the moment. Do you have any medical conditions I should know about?'

'No.'

'Diabetes, epilepsy?'

'Nothing.'

He was pulling up a vial now, chatting away as he flipped the bung on her IV access.

'Any chance you could be pregnant?'

'Not after the stunt you pulled a couple of weeks ago.' It was a vague attempt at humour as the foggy twilight world of pethidine descended, but Heath carried on talking, asking the questions. 'When was your last period, Isla? They're going to do a stack of X-rays when we get you to the hospital.'

'If you get me there.' Terrified eyes met his, finally admitting to herself her very real plight. The moments after the stretcher was removed would be the most critical time. If her injuries were serious, and from the way Heath was struggling to find a BP, from the giddy dots dancing in her eyes and the appalling dry mouth, Isla knew there was a fair chance they were, the moment the metal was removed her trauma would become apparent, and they both knew it.

'When was your last period, Isla?' Heath asked again, dodging the real issue.

'Dunno,' Isla mumbled, her eyes closing, sweet oblivion creeping in as the pethidine started working.

'Last week?'

'Dunno,' Isla mumbled again, but something in Heath's voice was dragging her back, forcing her to concentrate, to remember the last time she'd dragged the twins around the supermarket, blushing as Harry had pulled a pile of tampons off the shelf and Luke asking what they were for; to try and pinpoint when she'd scrabbled through the bathroom, tipped out her handbags in an attempt to find that one elusive tampon, to picture in her mind the last time she'd asked Sav to nip to the garage at some ungodly hour.

'You can buy them without milk, you know.'

'Sorry?'

'That's what the girl at the garage said to Sav. He bought a load of chocolate and about four litres of milk. He couldn't bring himself to just walk in and buy tampons.'

'When, Isla?' Heath pressed, and Isla closed her eyes.

'I don't know. I need Sav. Can he come in?'

Immediately Heath shook his head. 'We're going to get the side off. Once there's better access—'

'I need him, Heath.'

'Isla, I can't.'

'You have to.' Urgent eyes implored him. 'You have to, Heath, because you know as well as I do that once the side comes off, once the firefighters come in here with their gear, that could be it for me. He has to be here.'

'What if it's too much for him?'

She welcomed his honesty, stared at him through the darkness and prayed she might reach him.

'He can take it, Heath. He'll take it better being here with me than being left outside.'

'Ready, Doc?' Mike's voice boomed over the noise of the cutter revving up in the distance, and Isla held her breath.

'Not yet.' Heath put up his hand. 'Dr Ramirez is out there—the consultant. I think he's the one who should be here when they move the equipment. Could you have someone call him? Bring more blood in as well.'

'Thank you,' Isla whispered.

'Can I be godfather?' Heath grinned and then he did the nicest thing, slipped off his latex glove and held her hand, skin on skin as they waited for Sav to arrive. 'You'll be OK, Isla.'

'I have to be OK,' Isla gasped. 'I've got the twins…'

'And Sav,' Heath said, squeezing her hand harder. 'Here he is now.'

There was an appalling wait as Heath left her side, the confined space not enough for two, and Isla dragged on the oxygen and willed herself to stay calm as Heath gave a rapid handover to his senior. She felt more than heard Sav crawl towards her, her one free hand coiling into his as his hand closed around hers. Maybe her eyes had accustomed or perhaps it was a face she was used to seeing in the darkness, but every feature she needed to see was visible, from the dark, knowing eyes to the strong contours of his jaw, every vestige of reserve that had held her together disintegrating now as finally she didn't need to be brave, finally she could fall.

He was here.

Finally, she could just be.

'I can't remember when my last period was.'

Not the most romantic of greetings, but Sav understood, kissing the salty tears that sprang from her eyes, inhaling the scent of her hair as she lay there.

'I had that wine, that paˆteˊ, we went to that—'

'Hey!' Even as he spoke he was working, picking up her other arm and getting a second IV line into her. 'How many babies are conceived on the wedding night?' Somehow he smiled—somehow, just as he always did, when it really mattered he came up trumps.

'How much pâté, champagne and rotten mouldy cheese floats around then?'

'But—'

'Isla, you're worrying about listeria, foetal alcohol syndrome and a million maybes when the truth of the matter is that you've got a bloody stretcher wrapped around you.'

And it was so bizarre it was funny.

But that was Sav.

The one guy who could, in the most dire, the most vile circumstances make her smile.

'Remember when you were pregnant with the twins?' He was ripping a unit of blood out of its plastic case, squeezing it into her as he spoke. 'Remember how I had to hide the textbooks? You had everything from pre-eclampsia to thalassaemia and *you're* not even of Mediterranean origin.' She could hear a machine bleeping, watched as Sav tried not to frown. 'What the hell's Heath doing, putting on nasal prongs? I'm going to change you to a mask.'

'No!' It wasn't a shout, her breathing didn't

allow for that, but her voice was urgent. 'I want to talk, Sav.'

'Not now,' he said. 'Not now.'

'Yes, now,' Isla gasped, as Mike appeared again in the window.

'We're taking the dashboard off first instead of the side, Doc. We're getting the front passenger out first and then we'll be able to get better access to your patient.'

'No!' Sav shook his head fiercely. 'My…' He swallowed hard. 'This patient is bleeding, she's got a query pneumothorax, she needs to be freed first.'

'The other passenger has just lost consciousness. His respiration rate has gone right down and he's blown a pupil and needs urgent attention the doctor in charge says…'

'I'm the doctor in—' A squeeze on his hand held him back.

'Let them get Ted out,' Isla begged. 'Heath has to be the one to make the call, Sav. You're too close to be objective.'

'There's no such thing as too close, Isla,' Sav said softly. 'Not where we're concerned.'

And he was right.

Because closeness was the one thing that had been missing, and in the most dire of circumstances somehow they'd found it again when it had appeared to be lost for ever.

Closer perhaps than they'd ever been.

Lying in a hellhole, listening to the precarious task of extracting a critically ill patient who happened to be a friend, and colleague as well.

Ted.

As sick as Isla was right now, Ted was worse.

Harsh decisions, emergency triage, perhaps one of the toughest of all asks, because it wasn't figures you were shuffling, or deadlines you were trying to meet, but real lives and real outcomes that were being decided in limited time, with limited resources.

Not just who lived and who died—that would almost be too easy. The doctor in charge had, in that tiny slice of time, to assess a thousand different things.

Yes, Isla could go first, and maybe Ted would still live.

But a severe head injury without swift treatment would probably render him brain damaged, but with proper treatment, with the pressure on his brain relieved and adequate oxygenation, he might just walk out of the hospital, might just walk back into a life, a job and a family who needed him.

Whose condition needed the most rapid response was the tough call, and Sav couldn't be the one to make it.

'Talk to me,' Isla begged.

'I love you,' he soothed, but she shook her head.

'Please, Sav,' Isla gasped as they listened to the doctors and paramedics working, the urgent shouts for more blood, the snapping of metal as Ted was prised out. 'Talk to me.'

It felt like an age, but finally, almost imperceptibly he nodded, and if her oxygen saturation hadn't been on the wrong side of ninety per cent Isla would have held her breath, but no blessed machine bleeping was going to spoil this moment so she dragged the oxygen into her lungs and waited for him to finally tell her just how he was feeling.

'I miss him.' His face buried in her hair, his tears mingling with hers. 'Sometimes I feel better, sometimes I feel happy for a moment, and then I feel guilty—guilty for being OK, guilty for being able to smile when my little boy's dead. I still can't believe he's really gone.'

He isn't gone, she wanted to scream. She wanted to sob in his arms, wanted to wrap her arms around him and hold him tight, but all she had was her voice. 'He's there, he's everywhere, Sav, he's never going to leave us. I can still hear those songs he used to sing if I listen, hear those little giggles. I can smell him. He still makes me laugh. He isn't gone—as long as we keep him close he's here.'

'I just miss him so much.'

'I miss him, too,' Isla said. 'But I miss *you* as well, Sav, and so do the twins.' Her face crumpled, and the nasal prongs were not enough now, the tears so deep she needed every last bit of help just to breathe, not even resisting as Sav slipped the mask over her face. 'Oh, God, I just want to close my eyes and be with him but I love you all, too. I don't want us to separate…'

'But *you* went to a solicitor, Isla…'

'I didn't know what else to do,' Isla admitted. 'I wanted change, Sav, and I didn't know how else to get it.'

'We're coming now, Doc.' Mike's voice seemed to be coming through a fog, dragging them back to reality.

'Won't be long now.' Sav smiled down, but it faded midway. His face seemed to be blurring around the edges as he stared down at her, one hand held high above where she lay, squeezing the blood through. The blood-pressure machine alarm started as her blood pressure plummeted so dangerously low that it couldn't pick up a reading. Sav pulled on his stethoscope, used the old method, as Heath had.

'I need her out.' Sav's voice was urgent. 'I need help in here now!'

And it should have been scary, should have been the most frightening time of her life, but inexplicably it wasn't. She'd been through more pain than any mother ever should, nothing could now hurt her. And she'd never felt more tired. Sav's beautiful face wasn't quite enough to keep her eyes open. It would be so much easier to say goodbye to the pain and the agony, the sweet thought of just closing her eyes, of seeing Casey, her baby, her little boy, just a tiny step away.

'I never wanted to leave you,' she whispered, her voice almost resigned, but Sav was having none of it, his fingers gripping her cheeks, his voice harsh with emotion as he dragged her back.

'Stay, then.' Sav's eyes bored into hers, forcing her to focus, to listen, to hold on. 'Stay with me, stay with not just me but with Luke and Harry, because, my God, Isla, we need you so much. Stay,' he said again. 'And I'll do every last thing I can to put the "happy" back into our marriage.

'I love you, Isla.'

And he did.

She'd known that all along.

'Stay,' he said again.

And she mouthed the word 'yes'.

Not because she had to, but because she wanted to. Because life was precious and short and sweet and, despite the pain, despite the torture, it was the most precious gift of all.

'Theatre's on standby?' Sav checked as Heath climbed into the newly created slightly wider space.

With the passenger seat removed, the task of extricating the stretcher was, as Mike had predicted, easier now.

But it was the most dangerous moment for Isla.

Once the pressure was removed, she could bleed out in a matter of seconds. The stretcher that was trapping her was also possibly saving her, and no one knew this more than Sav.

'From here straight to the theatre table if necessary,' Heath confirmed. 'Everyone's on standby in Resus. By the sound of it everyone in the hospital, full stop, is on standby. Once we get her out, we'll assess…'

His voice was drowned out as the cutter started up again, Heath holding Isla's head steady as Sav held her hand, whispering into her ear, all the while trying to drown out the horrific noise with words of love and encouragement as they worked to free her.

'Hold it.' Lifting up his hand in command, Mike ordered one of his firefighters to stop cutting and the appalling, teeth-rattling noise faded as Mike again assessed the twisted metal wrapped around Isla. 'It's free.'

'Right, no one moves till I say so,' Sav ordered, and for once Heath didn't argue. Sav was a leader and, right or wrong, he was leading now, and nothing Heath was going to say would stop him.

'Heath, ready with the chest tube if she needs it?' He didn't wait for a nod as he turned his attention to the firefighter. 'Once we've lifted the stretcher, get it out and let us work. Be ready to squeeze through the blood.'

'Got it.' Mike nodded, checking for the umpteenth time the position of the stretcher, talking to his men about their ensuing movements, taking one final look around the confined area, assessing every last detail in an attempt to ensure the lift was as swift and as easy for Isla as possible. 'We're going to lift the stretcher directly up and then over your heads, Docs, and then it will be behind you. You'll have to move forward a bit on my say-so, so that we can lower it, but you'll have more room at the patient's side.'

'Got it!' Sav nodded, his voice steady, his hand squeezing Isla's, but despite the brave smile she could see the fear in his eyes.

'Ready, Doc?'

'Hold on.' And if it was against protocol that he was in there, Sav didn't give a damn. There was nothing Mike could do now anyway, maybe put in a complaint somewhere down the line, but somewhere down the line seemed a distant dream right now. 'Hang in there, Isla,' Sav whispered, kissing the pale, cold cheek, noting with infinite relief the tiny flicker of her eyelashes. 'I love you, the boys love you.'

He gave the nod, held his breath as the stretcher rose. He ached to get to her, but knew he had to wait just a little bit longer as the firefighters skilfully extricated the metal, lifted it up from Isla's body and over Sav's and Heath's heads. They inched forward when they could to finally be by her side.

'Her air entry's better.' Heath's stethoscope was over her chest as Sav did a rapid assessment of Isla's other injuries. Her stomach was bruised and distended, but her pelvis was thankfully stable, her reflexes appropriate. And even if it wasn't great it was a helluva lot better than he had feared—he had been terrified that her chest injuries were serious, that her lungs might have filled with blood the second the stretcher lifted, that all that would be left for him to do was hold her. 'Possible fractured sternum,' Heath added, palpating her chest wall. 'But no flail chest.'

'She's bleeding out in her abdomen.' Sav's voice was amazingly controlled. 'We need to get her out, stat.'

And they did.

The heroics they had prepared for didn't need to be put into action. Isla needed more blood, more oxygen, but most of all she needed to be in Theatre.

Sav held her head, commanding from the top, keeping her neck in line as hands lifted her slowly out to the waiting stretcher, oblivious to the crowds gathered on the pavement being kept back by the police. Only as they lowered her onto the stretcher and wheeled her to the waiting ambulance did he finally let go and allow Heath to take over. Quite simply, he couldn't do it any more, couldn't be her doctor for another minute, just needed to be her husband.

'Into Resus, guys!' Heath was giving the orders, pushing the blood through as the ambulance tore through the streets, sirens from the police escort mingling with the ambulance's own, the speed that had almost killed her the only thing that could save her now. And not one person present gave it a thought. The sole mission was to get Isla where she
needed to be.

It was Sav's turn now to glimpse Isla's hell.

To sit in a bland, beige interview room and not have a clue what was going on. To brace yourself at every footstep, to choke back tears as the door opened and a quick glimpse and a kiss was all you could get as they raced her up to Theatre.

To finally pick up the telephone and make the calls.

CHAPTER FOURTEEN

'HEY!' Dark eyes smiled gently down at her, that beautiful expressive mouth trembling into a tender smile as slowly the world came back into focus. 'What took you so long?'

'Sav!' Tears were filling in Isla's eyes as realization crept in. Appalled, not just at what she'd been through but Sav, too, and the boys. 'The boys—'

'Are fine,' Sav broke in. 'I went home and told them and they've been in to see you, but just for a moment.'

'They've been here?'

It was too much, much too much. The thought of Luke and Harry seeing her like this, the fear they must be going through, but Sav understood her concerns without her even having to voice them. 'I told them very gently, I told them you were going to be OK, but they really needed to see you for themselves.'

She gave a tiny, glum nod of understanding, screwing her eyes closed against the tears but opening them again as Sav tentatively continued.

'I figured after what happened with…with Casey, they wouldn't believe you were OK till they saw you for themselves. I'll bring them back in the morning.'

And, he'd said it, had said the one word she'd needed to hear, the one word that would keep Casey alive for all of them. Her eyes filled with emotion and
gratitude as his hand tightened around hers.

'How's Ted?'

'Doing well,' Sav answered. 'They got him straight into Resus and made a burr hole. He had a large blood clot pressing on his brain, but they got it out in time. He's still heavily sedated, but his responses are good and they're pretty optimistic he'll be OK.'

'Physically perhaps.' Isla shrugged. 'We couldn't do anything for Doug, we just had to lie there and listen.' Tears trickled down her sore, swollen cheeks into her hair, matted still with blood, but as Sav stared down at her, he could only think that she'd never looked more beautiful.

'How do you feel?' he asked gruffly, clearly awkward at having taken the giant step forward and saying Casey's name.

'Sore.'

'That's what happens when you go hurtling around in an ambulance,' Sav teased lightly, then his voice grew more serious. 'You had a lacerated liver, Isla. That's what all the blood loss was from. I know a lacerated liver isn't exactly fun, but the surgeons repaired it and you are going to be OK, which is a lot better than it could have been. For a while in there it looked as if the bleeding might have been…'

'From my chest?'

Sav gave a small nod, his eyes closing for a

second in horror at what could have been. 'You've been lucky.'

'I don't feel very lucky.' Her voice wobbled, tears breaking into the strong façade she'd almost created. 'Why us?'

It was the first time she'd said it, the first time she'd given in to her anger at the world, a world that just seemed to keep dishing it out. 'Why do these things happen to us, Sav?'

There was no response to that, not really. Isla knew it but, not for the first time, Sav surprised her, came up with an answer when she'd have sworn there wasn't one.

'Because we can take it,' he said softly. 'Because we're stronger than we think. Sometimes it might be me leaning on you, Isla, and sometimes it will be the other way round, but together we can take whatever the world throws at us. Who knows? Maybe good times are just around the corner.'

'Maybe,' Isla mumbled, not entirely convinced, but there was an urgency in her voice as she turned her head to face him. 'I'm sorry for going to see a solicitor, Sav, sorry you had to find out from Heath. I still can't really believe that I went.'

'Let's just put it behind us, shall we?'

'Can you?' Isla asked, finally relaxing a touch as he gave a slow, definite nod, but an attempt at a cough caused more pain than she'd have thought possible.

'You've got a fractured sternum, too,' Sav added, as if it was just another item on the shopping list of pain. 'That's why it hurts so much to cough.'

'Anything else?' Isla sighed, resting back on her pillow, tired, so tired all of a sudden.

'A few bruises,' Sav carried on, 'a nasty cut on your cheek, but the plastic surgeons sutured it, they've done a great job...' His voice was in the distance, lulling her off to sleep as the list grew ever longer. 'And the baby's still hanging in there.'

'Baby?' Her eyes snapped open. She was very much awake now, struggling to sit up and coughing violently, horror drenching her as she recalled the forgotten conversation in the ambulance as Heath had tried to get her to remember the date of her last period.

'Lie back,' Sav soothed, gently pushing her shoulders down, waiting for the racking cough to abate, for her to catch her breath and calm down. But there was absolutely no hope of calming down with what Sav said next. 'A big baby!' Tears were swimming in those gorgeous expressive eyes of his, a smile breaking out on that tired, strained face that had been through so much. He gazed down at his wife, moved a touch closer on the side of the bed to hold her gently as he carried on talking. 'You're nearly halfway there, Isla, eighteen to nineteen weeks.'

'Oh, no, all that running, the accident...! That's terrible...' Panic, utter panic flooded her, but Sav was holding her, soothing her, reassuring her, as only Sav could.

'That's good,' he said firmly. 'That means you're past the first trimester, well past it actually, and the baby's that much bigger and stronger.'

'How, though?' she begged. 'How could I not have known? I don't even have a bump.'

'You do, Isla.' His hand gently moved hers to her abdomen, carefully avoiding the painful scar from her surgery. 'Not a very big one, admittedly, but there's a little life going on in there, and it would seem it's determined to hang in, despite the odds.'

She *did* have a bump. Isla could feel the small wedge of muscle as her hand tentatively pushed down. Oh, nothing like she'd had with the twins, nothing like she'd had with Casey, but there beneath her fingers were the first tiny glimmers of hope she'd felt in a long while.

'How could I not have known?' Isla whispered. 'Nineteen weeks, I mean. I'm nineteen weeks pregnant and I didn't even know.'

'I've spoken to Declan, the obstetrician,' Sav added. 'And apparently it's not that abnormal. For some women who've lost a child, it's easier to bury facts than to face them, and if you don't believe the psychological take on things, maybe you just had too much going on in that crazy head of yours to take it in.' He watched her blink in surprise, that face, still pretty despite the bruises and scar, shaking on the pillow as she tried to take it all in. 'I think you did know, Isla.'

She shook her head angrily, appalled that he might think she would hide something like this from him, but Sav pressed on.

'Not consciously, of course, but somewhere deep inside I think you knew that things had to change. And you were right. I have shut you out, Isla. Things had to come to a head if we were going to give a new baby the love and devotion it deserves. Maybe that's why you went to see a solicitor…'

It made sense.

For the first time the world actually made sense.

'I'll never tell him, of course,' Sav said, 'but Heath actually did us both a favour.'

'He was great at the accident.' Isla dragged

her mind away from her own problems for a moment and thought about the man who had taken his gloves off and held her hand when the world had been so scary. 'He was great, Sav. Heath really is a good doctor. Maybe he just lost his way a little bit.'

'I can understand that.' Sav nodded. 'He was devastated when his wife left him and I guess losing out on the consultant's position only made him feel worse. Anyway, he came good in the end, which is just as well, considering what's around the corner for him.'

'A consultant's position?' Isla frowned. 'But there isn't room for another. You said—'

'Acting consultant,' Sav corrected her. 'For a few months at least, and then when we get back, if he's done a good job, I'll make damn sure that Martin makes room for him.'

'Get back?' Drugs, pain, emotion, exhaustion were all creeping in now, making it impossible to keep up, her eyes so heavy she had to struggle to keep them open.

'Where are we going?'

'To Spain,' Sav whispered, kissing her eyes closed, talking softly all the while. 'When you're well enough, I'm going to take some long service leave. We'll fly your mum and dad out and we're all going to stay at my parents', soak in the sun, eat more than we should, fish with the boys and talk. Talk about us and about Casey and how much we love him and how we're going to get better...' She didn't know if she was awake or asleep, if this was all some delicious dream. 'We're going to have our *bebé* in Spain—a little *muchacha* or *muchacho*. I don't care which, boy or girl will be wonderful.'

It sounded wonderful.

No need to open her eyes, no need to do anything except lie there with Sav holding her and picture a dream that might, just might become a reality. But one thing was troubling her, one little thing that she had to know before she finally closed her eyes and slept.

'Sav.' Peeling her eyes open, she squinted to focus. He was still there, still smiling softly down at her, still loving her as he always, always would.

'What's Spanish for push?'

EPILOGUE

EMPUJE.

It would stay in her mind for ever.

'*Empuje*, Isla.'

'*No puedo*,' she'd said over and over, screaming it louder and louder, but either she'd got her words muddled up or no one had really been listening. 'I can't!' she'd groaned to the enthusiastic midwives and doctor. 'It's too hard. *Mas fuerte!*'

Sitting on the veranda, or *mirador* as Sav's mum called it, Isla stared at the dark mass of curls, the little pink face snuggled into her breast, scarcely able to believe she was really here.

And not just that her daughter was finally here, not just that she was holding little Sophia to breasts that ached to feed, in arms that ached to hold a child, but that she was here in Sav's home, happy, really happy, sitting watching the late afternoon sun dipping to the horizon, the sparkling Mediterranean Sea glittering before her. And undoubtedly most beautiful of all, Sav wandering back along a sandy dusty path, Harry firmly entrenched on his shoulders as Luke ran ahead, clutching a handful of fish.

They missed him.

Every moment of every day they missed Casey, and Sophia couldn't, didn't fill that gap, nothing ever would.

Isla knew and always would, as Sav wandered back with his sons, that there should be another little guy racing ahead, or ambling behind, a head of auburn curls catching the sun.

But there wasn't.

And they were learning to live with it.

Learning to hold on to each other through the dark times and embrace the good times.

Good times.

'We've sold a fish!' Luke was so excited he

could barely get the words out, his sun-kissed body covered in sand, his smile as wide as his face. 'Señora Casta said they needed extra *pes—pes—pescados* for the restaurant tonight.

'That means fish,' he added, proudly holding up a fistful of notes. 'We're going to count it, see how much we've made. Come on, Harry!'

Harry jumped off Sav's shoulders and popped a quick kiss on the top of Sophia's head and an even quicker one in the vague direction of Isla's cheek, before following his brother excitedly inside, the last few weeks in Spain having served not only to bring him out of his shell but propelling him at full speed into the wonderful, carefree world that a seven-year-old should inhabit, and Harry was embracing it.

'They've had a great day.' Sav grinned.

'It sounds it.' Isla laughed. 'Did you set it up?'

'No!' Sav said, but his eyes were on Sophia, waiting patiently for Isla to finish burping her then holding his arms out for a long-awaited cuddle with his daughter. 'They really did want more fish. We only had one that was big enough for her to buy, but the boys are delighted! Guess where they want to go tomorrow?' He groaned, but it was a feeble protest. Every other part of him was smiling.

'Where's everyone?'

'Gone for a walk. I can't believe how well they all get on!'

'Great, isn't it?' Sav nodded. 'I'm sure any other family would break out in a cold sweat at the thought of having both sets of in-laws living with them for a while, but it's worked out wonderfully, hasn't it? Your dad's looking really well.'

'We're all looking really well,' Isla agreed, standing up and fixing her sarong then staring down at her daughter, nestled against Sav's bronzed chest. 'Who does she look like Sav?' Isla asked for the hundredth time as they both gazed at their creation.

'Well, she's got my hair,' Sav mused, 'Luke's ears, Harry's suspicious eyes and I reckon she's got Casey's smile.'

'What about me?' Isla pouted, but inside her heart soared. Casey's name peppered the conversation so much more easily now. 'There's surely a bit of me in there—I am her mother after all!'

'Nope.' Sav shrugged. 'I can't see it. I guess I'm just going to have to trust you on that one.

'Now, on to more serious things. We've got four babysitters lined up so how about you and I take a wander down to Sen̄ora Casta's tonight, try some of that fish we caught, have a bottle of sangria…?'

'Sounds wonderful,' Isla sighed.

'Great. I'll go and put Sophia down for a sleep then have a shower before you hog it.' A slow lazy kiss found her lips and she revelled in it. Revelled in his strong arm around her shoulders, that delicious full mouth exploring hers as their baby snuggled between them.

'Dad!'

An indignant wail from inside broke the moment, and Isla sat back down as Sav went in to break up whatever had broken out, watching idly as the postman cycled up then made his way over. Already familiar with Isla's appalling lack of Spanish, he spoke in broken English as Isla stared up at him, shielding her eyes from the low sun with her hand.

'Dr Ramirez.' He held out a parcel. 'I need… *firma*.' He held out a pen. 'Dr Ramirez, he need…'

'He's in the shower,' Isla said apologetically. 'Maybe I can help.'

And the poor postman must have thought she was the most emotionally unstable, labile woman in history because as she took the pen her eyes filled with tears suddenly, her lip wobbling as the words came out. She was realizing, not for the first time, how different things could have been, the fragile world they'd inhabited for a while, and how proud and happy she was to be able to say what came next.

'Maybe I can help,' she started again, accepting the parcel and lifting the pen to sign.

'I'm Dr Ramirez's wife.'

MEDICAL ROMANCE™

Large Print

Titles for the next six months...

October

THE DOCTOR'S RESCUE MISSION   Marion Lennox
THE LATIN SURGEON   Laura MacDonald
DR CUSACK'S SECRET SON   Lucy Clark
HER SURGEON BOSS   Abigail Gordon

November

HER EMERGENCY KNIGHT   Alison Roberts
THE DOCTOR'S FIRE RESCUE   Lilian Darcy
A VERY SPECIAL BABY   Margaret Barker
THE CHILDREN'S HEART SURGEON   Meredith Webber

December

THE DOCTOR'S SPECIAL TOUCH   Marion Lennox
CRISIS AT KATOOMBA HOSPITAL   Lucy Clark
THEIR VERY SPECIAL MARRIAGE   Kate Hardy
THE HEART SURGEON'S PROPOSAL   Meredith Webber

MILLS & BOON®

Live the emotion

0905 LP 2P P1 Medical

MEDICAL ROMANCE™

Large Print

MILLS & BOON®

Live the emotion

0905 LP 2P P2 Medical